A BRAWL BEFORE THE BENCH

Star Levitt sat very still. Suddenly the rage that was in him exploded to madness. He leaped from his chair and sprang for Canavan.

Levitt's swinging right caught Canavan on the cheekbone and he staggered. Canavan braced himself but Levitt came in swinging with both fists. Canavan buried a right in his midsection, then hooked a bone-jarring left to the face.

Suddenly Levitt abandoned slugging. Clasping his hands behind Canavan's back he ground his knuckles into Canavan's spine. Canavan felt a stab of excruciating pain and fell backward, bringing Levitt down on top of him.

Both men got up and Canavan moved in fast. Levitt's breath was coming in great gasps. A right split his cheek, a left widened the cut.

Suddenly, Levitt turned and leaped through the window into the alley.

WHERE
THE LONG
GRASS BLOWS

Louis L'Amour

WHERE THE LONG GRASS BLOWS
A Bantam Book / November 1976

ISBN 0–553–10286–9

Published simultaneously in the United States and Canada

Chapter I

There was a lonely place where the trail ran up to the sky, turning sharply away at the rimrock where a man could see all the valley below, a splendid green of forest and meadow fading into the purple of the farther mountains. It was a place where a man could look down upon eagles, soaring far below, yet thousands of feet above the valley's floor. Here at sundown a man came riding.

Bill Canavan rode a horse strangely marked, a true leopard Appaloosa . . . white with black spots except for a splash of blue roan on the left hip. He drew up where the trail turned, and sat his saddle, looking over the valley below. The gelding, nostrils spreading to catch whatever scent there was, pricked its ears and looked eagerly toward the wide valley below.

The rider was a tall man, narrow of hip and broad of shoulder, his features blunt and rugged, not handsome but strong. There was a tough, confident look about him, and he looked upon this valley now as Cortez might have looked when first he saw the Valley of Mexico.

Bill Canavan came alone, but he did not come seeking favors, nor even work. He came as a conqueror.

For Bill Canavan had made his decision. At twenty-seven he was sitting in the middle of all he owned, a splendid Appaloosa gelding, a fine California saddle of hand-tooled leather, a .44 Winchester rifle and two walnut-butted Colt .44 pistols. These were his all. Behind him was a life that began with birth in a covered wagon rolling westward, a boyhood in the gold and silver boom camps of California, Nevada, Montana and Colorado, a cattle-drive over the Chisholm Trail, another over the Goodnight-Loving Trail, shotgun guard on a stage and scouting Indians for the Army.

He had fought rustlers and Kiowas, Comanches and Apaches, Sioux and Blackfeet, with nothing to show for it but a few scars here and there and his memories of hunger, thirst, cold, of hard winters and dry range and long dusty drives. All it had brought him was trouble and hard riding. Now his decision was made. He was going to ride for himself and fight for himself.

His cool dark eyes scanned the valley below, and his appreciation of terrain would have done credit to a general. And in his own way he was a general, and his arrival was an invasion, yet the only force he commanded was himself.

Bill Canavan was a young man with a plan. He wanted not wealth but a ranch, a well-watered ranch in good stock country, and he intended to settle for nothing less. The fact that he was down to his last three dollars meant nothing, for his mind was made up. And back down the trail there were men who could tell you that Bill Canavan with his mind set on something was a force with which to reckon.

Yet he was not riding blindly into a strange land. For, like the tactician he was, he had gathered his information carefully, judged the situation, the terrain, the time and the people, and now he was ready.

This was new country, but he knew the landmarks and the personalities. He knew the strengths and weaknesses of its rulers, knew the economic factors of their existence, knew the stresses and strains within it. He knew that he rode into a valley at war, that blood had been shed and that armed men rode its trails night and day. Into this maelstrom he rode, a man alone, determined to have his own from the country.

The wolves were at war over the carcass of the land, and he, a stranger, fiercer predator, was moving to the attack.

He turned the gelding away from the rim and started down the trail through the pines, a trail soon to be dark, a trail somber, majestic in its stillness under the columned trees.

As he rode into the trees he removed his hat and slowed his horse to a walk. It was a good country, a country in which a man could live and grow, and where if he was fortunate he might have sons to grow tall and straight beside him.

This was what he wished for. No longer did he look for far horizons. He wanted his own hearth fire, the creak of his own pump, the heads of his own horses looking over the gate bars for his hand to feed them. He wanted peace, and seeking it he had come to a land at war.

A faint smell of woodsmoke drew his attention to the edge of the meadow. He drew up, then walked his horse over to where the fire had been. The earth was much trampled and the grass torn. Studying the scene, his attention held for an instant on a blackened ring at one side and back from the fire.

His eyes glinted with hard humor. "A cinch-ring artist," he said to the gelding, "dropped her there to

cool and singed the grass." A pretty handy man, no
doubt, but not a wise one. A smarter or less confident
man would have pulled up that handful of blackened
grass and thrown it into the fire.

There had been two men here, his eyes told him.
Two men and two horses. A big man with small feet
. . . the impressions were deeper and he had mounted
the largest horse.

He studied the scene. This was a new country
for him and it behooved a man to understand the
local customs. He grinned at the thought. If cinch-ring
branding was one of the local customs, it was an
unusual one. In most parts of the country it was an
invitation to a hanging. The cinch-ring artist was
apt to find himself at the wrong end of a rope with
nothing under his feet.

The procedure was simple enough. One took a
cinch-ring from his own saddle gear and, holding it
with a couple of sticks—after it was red-hot, of
course—he used it like any other branding iron. A good
hand with a cinch-ring could easily duplicate any
known brand, depending only on his degree of skill.

Bill Canavan glanced around. If he were found
on the spot it would require explaining, and at the
moment he had no intention of explaining anything.
Swinging the gelding, he rode down the trail once
more.

Not three miles away lay the cowtown known as
Soledad. To his right, and about six miles away, was
an imposing cluster of buildings shaded beneath a fine
grove of old cottonwoods. Somewhat nearer and also
shaded was a somewhat smaller ranch.

Beyond the rocky ridge that stretched an anxious
finger into the lush valley was Walt Pogue's Box N
spread.

The farther ranch belonged to Charlie Reynolds;
his CR brand was the largest in the area. The nearer
ranch belonged to Tom and Dixie Venable.

"When thieves fall out," he said aloud, "honest men get their dues. Or so they say. Without laying any claim to being more than average honest, I've got a hunch I'll be around to pick up the pieces. There's trouble coming, and when the smoke of battle blows away I'll be top-dog on one of those ranches.

"They have it all. They have range, money, power. They have gunhands riding for them, but you and me, Rio, we've only got each other."

Down there the wolves ran in packs, but he would circle the packs alone, and when the moment came, he would move in.

"There's an old law, Rio, that only the strong survive. Those ranches are held by men who were strong. Some of them still are. They were strong enough to take the land from smaller, weaker men. That's the story of Reynolds and Pogue. They rustled cows until they grew big enough and now they sit on the housetops and crow. Or they did until they began fighting each other."

"Your reasoning," the cool voice behind him was feminine, "is logical, but dangerous. I would suggest that if you must talk to your horse you be sure his are the only ears present!"

She sat well in the saddle, poised and alert. There was a quirk of humor at the corners of her mouth, and nothing of coyness or fear in her manner. Every inch of her breathed of quality, but a quality underlaid with both fire and steel.

"That's good advice," he said. "It's a bad habit a man gets into, talkin' to his horse. Comes of riding alone too much."

He was looking at her with very real appreciation. Women of any kind were scarce, but such women as this—

"Now that you've looked me over," she suggested cooly, "would you like to examine my teeth for age?"

He was not embarrassed. "No, ma'am. Now that I've looked you over I'd say you're pretty much of a woman. The kind of a woman who's made for a man!"

She smiled, obviously pleased, but she changed the subject. "Just which ranch are you thinking about? Where do you intend to be top-dog when the fighting is over?"

"Well, now. I haven't rightly made up my mind. I'm a right choosy man when it comes to horses, ranches and women!"

"Yes?" She glanced at the gelding. "I'd say your judgment of horses isn't obvious by that one. Not that he isn't a beauty, but I think you could do better. I never did favor those off-colored horses."

"I doubt if I could do better," Canavan said. "And I'd bet a little money he could outrun that beauty of yours, here to Soledad."

Her eyes flashed. "You're an idiot. Flame is the fastest horse in this country! He comes of racing stock!"

"He's a fine horse, but I'd bet my saddle against a hundred dollars that my Appaloosa will kick dust in his face before we get to Soledad."

There was scorn in her laughter. "You're on!" she said, and her red horse gave a great bound and hit the trail running. That jump gave the bay a start, but Bill knew his gelding.

"Come on, boy! We've got to beat that horse! We need the money!" Rio, seeming as always to understand, stretched his legs and ran like a scared rabbit.

As they swept into the main road, and into full sight of Soledad, the bay was leading by three lengths. But despite the miles behind it, the Appaloosa loved to run and he was running now.

The gelding had the blood of Arabians in his veins, and he was used to rough country and the off-hand style of cow camp racing. The road took a small jog but Bill Canavan did not take the horse around. Instead, he cut through the rocks and mesquite and hit the road scarcely a length behind the big red horse.

In Soledad, men were coming out into the street now, watching the racers come toward them. With a half mile to go the red horse was slowing. He was a sprinter, but he had been living well with too little running, while the gelding was just beginning to run. Neck stretched out, the gelding ran hard and Canavan leaned far forward to cut the wind resistance and lend some impetus with his weight. The mustang pulled up alongside the bay horse, and neck and neck they raced up to the town. With the nearest building only a few jumps ahead, Canavan spoke to the Appaloosa.

"*Now*, Rio! *Now!*"

With a lunge the spotted horse was past and went racing into the street, leading by a length.

Canavan eased up and let his horse run down the street abreast of the red horse. They slowed to a canter, then a walk. The girl's eyes were wide and angry.

"You cheated! You cut across the bend!"

He chuckled. "You could have, ma'am. You got off to a running start, left me standing still!"

"I thought you wanted a race!" she said scornfully. "You cheated!"

Bill Canavan pulled up sharply, his eyes hard. "Obviously, ma'am, you come from a long line of sportsmen! You can forget the bet!"

The sarcasm cut like a whip. She opened her mouth to speak, suddenly ashamed of the way she had acted. After all, she had taken advantage at the start, and it was only fair—

He had turned his horse away and was walking off down the street, and for an instant she was about to follow. Impatiently, she tossed her head. Let him go, she thought . . . who does he think he is, anyway?

Yet she turned once more to look back. Who *was* he, anyway?

Chapter II

Several men were standing in front of the livery stable when he rode up. They looked first at his horse, and then at him. "That's a runner you've got there, stranger! I reckon Dixie Venable didn't relish gettin' beat! She sets store by that Flame horse, treats him like a baby!"

"It's a damn fine horse," Canavan replied. "He just needs more work."

He led the horse into the stable, rubbed him down and fed him. As he worked he turned the situation over in his mind. The girl had been Dixie Venable, one of the owners of the VV spread, and she had heard him thinking aloud about his plans. How seriously she would take either him or his plans was another thing, but it did not matter. He had come to the Valley ready for trouble, and the sooner they understood it the better.

Yet the beauty of the girl stuck in his mind when

all else was dismissed—not only her beauty but also her pride and fire. She was something different, something he had never seen in a woman before. Not that his experience had been all that great. When a man works on cow ranches and cattle drives, his chances at feminine companionship can be limited. Even when he drove stage or rode shotgun, the girls were all on the inside and he was outside where the action was.

He was conscious of approaching footsteps that stopped beside him. For a moment he continued to work, but the man did not move on. Canavan straightened up and looked around into a broad, handsome face. The man was smiling. He thrust out a large hand.

"My name's Walt Pogue. I own the Box N. Is that horse for sale?"

"No, he's not."

"Figured he wasn't, but if you change your mind come looking for me. I'll give you five hundred for him."

Five hundred? That was a lot of money for a horse in a country full of ten dollar mustangs, and where a horse was often traded for a quart of whiskey.

"No," he repeated, "he's not for sale."

"Lookin' for work? I could use a hand."

Bill Canavan stood erect again and looked at Pogue across the horse's back. He noticed, and the thought somehow irritated him, that Pogue was even bigger than himself. The rancher was all of three inches taller and forty pounds heavier, and he did not look fat.

"Gun hand?" he asked cooly. "Or cowhand?"

Walt Pogue's eyes changed a little, hardening ever so slightly. "Why, mostly that would depend on you, but if you hire on as a warrior you'd have to be good!"

"I'm good. As good as anybody you've got."

"As good as Bob Streeter or Rep Hanson?"

Bill Canavan's expression did not change, but

within him something tightened up ever so slightly. If Pogue had hired Streeter and Hanson this was going to be ugly. Both were killers, and not particular how they killed.

"As good as Streeter or Hanson?" he shrugged. "A couple of cheap killers. Blood hunters. They aren't fighting men."

His dark eyes held the searching stare of Walt Pogue again. "Who does Reynolds have?"

Pogue's face seemed to lower a little, like a charging bull. He stared back at Canavan. "He's got Emmett Chubb."

Emmett Chubb!

So? And after all these years? "He won't have him long," Canavan said, "because I'm going to kill him."

Triumph shone in Pogue's eyes. Swiftly he moved around the horse. "Mister," he said quietly, "that job could get you an even thousand dollars!"

"I don't take money for killing snakes."

"You do that job within three days and you'll get a thousand dollars!" Pogue replied. "My word on it."

Bill Canavan slapped Rio on the hip and walked past the big man without another glance and went to the street. Three men sat on the hitching rail near the stable door. Had they heard what was said inside? He doubted it, and yet the thought disturbed him. In a hard land where hard men lived, there had been many fights and he'd had his share of them, but he was not a killer for hire and did not want the reputation. He would take Emmett Chubb in his own good time.

Across the street and three doors down was the Trail Emporium. For a moment his eyes held on the one light gleaming at the back of the store. It was after-hours and the place was closed, but if he went to the back door there might be a chance. Deliberately he crossed the street and went toward the light.

Behind him Walt Pogue moved into the big doorway and stared after him, his brow furrowed with thought. His eyes watched the lean, powerful figure of the stranger as he crossed the street with a puzzled expression. Who was the man? Where had he come from? Why was he here?

Pogue had noticed the guns—well-polished handles and tied-down guns, although many a gunfighter did not bother with that, and men wore their guns wherever it suited them, and with no prescribed pattern. But this fellow had the remote eyes and the careful eyes of a man who had lived much with danger. He had refused the offer of a job . . . or had he merely avoided the question for now? Yet he had been aware of conditions in the Valley, and had immediately wished to know why he was being hired . . . *if* he consented to work.

Had Reynolds sent for him? Or Tom Venable? He had come into town, racing with Dixie. Had they met on the trail, or had they come from the VV? That was something Pogue wanted to know, and at once. If Tom Venable was hiring gunhands it would mean trouble of another sort, and that he did not want. One thing at a time.

Where was Canavan going now? Resisting an instinct to follow the stranger, Pogue turned and walked up the street to the Bit and Bridle Saloon. Yet he paused at the door, thinking. Whatever was done now must be done quickly, for there was too much at stake. Still, if this newcomer would eliminate Emmett Chubb, even put him out of action for a while, matters would be vastly more simple. The more he thought of that, the more he liked it. Hold off, he told himself, let his offer of a thousand dollars work on this stranger. If he was half as good as he seemed to think he was, he might just take Chubb out of action, and that would leave Reynolds seriously handicapped.

He went on into the saloon and ordered a drink, mulling over possible moves. The thought returned to his mind, the thought that kept recurring. Maybe he and Reynolds were damned fools to get into this fight, yet pride would not let him back off . . . pride and the chance to achieve what he wished.

In the alley back of the Emporium, Bill Canavan approached the back door. Twice he paused to look back and to listen, but he heard nothing. It was Pogue who worried him. For a moment he had thought the big man would attempt to follow him, and he'd been ready. He stepped up to the door and tapped lightly.

Footsteps sounded from within, and he heard a faint whisper of sound that could have been a gun being drawn from a scabbard. "Who's there?"

"A rider from the Pecos," Canavan said softly.

The door opened at once and Canavan slipped through the opening. The man who stood facing him with a drawn gun was plump now, and white-haired, yet the eyes were not old eyes; they were shrewd and knowing.

"Coffee?"

"Sure. And something to eat if there's anything around."

"About to eat, myself." The man placed the gun on the sideboard and took the coffee pot from the stove, filling two cups as Bill Canavan dropped into a chair. He went to the stove and took the frying pan and broke eggs into it. "Who sent you?"

"An old friend of yours heard I was headed this way. He said if I needed a smart man who could give me some information or advice to look you up. And he told me what to say."

"My days on that trail are over. I've got a nice business and I like it here. I don't know what you want, but it's likely you've come to the wrong place."

"You said your days on that trail were over. Well, mine never started. This is a business trip. I am planning to locate in the Valley."

"Locate *here?* Well, you came for advice, and you'll get it. Get on your horse and ride out of here as fast as you can. This is a rough country for strangers and there have been too many of them around lately. Things are due to bust wide open and there will be a sight of killing before it's over."

"You're right, of course."

"And when it's over, what's left for a gun hand? You can go on the owl-hoot . . . ride the outlaw trail until somebody shoots you, or they hang you. The very man who hired you and paid you warrior's wages won't have anything to do with you once the shooting's over.

"There's a revolution brewing in the Valley, and if you know anything about the history of revolutions you'll recall that as soon as the revolution is over they liquidate the revolutionaries. You take my advice and ride out of here . . . now."

The older man was right, of course. To ride out would be the intelligent, sensible and safe course, but he had absolutely no intention of doing it.

"Scott, I didn't come here to hire on as a gun hand, although I've already had an offer from Pogue. I came in here because I've sized it up and know what it's like. This country is wide open for a good man, a strong man. There's room for me here, and I mean to take it. I want a ranch of my own, Scott, and I plan to get mine the same way Pogue, Reynolds and all the others got theirs."

"You mean with a gun?" Scott tipped the frying pan and pushed eggs onto a plate for him. "You're crazy! Pogue has at least thirty men on his range, most of them paid warriors. Reynolds has just about as many, and maybe more. And you come in here alone . . . Or are you alone?"

Scott stared at him, hard-eyed. "You ain't bringin' an army in here, are you, son? There'll be killing enough without that."

"I'm alone, Scott, and I won't need any help. I'll either make it or I'll get killed. All my life, Scott, I've been fighting for existence. I've fought to protect the cattle of other men, fought for the homes of other men. I've ridden shotgun protecting bullion that belonged to other men. I've fought and worked; I've eaten dust and sweat and blood. Now I want something for myself."

Scott helped himself to some eggs and fried potatoes and sat down across the table from Canavan. He knew just how Bill Canavan felt, for until a few years ago he had felt much that way himself. He'd even taken the wrong route, rustling and robbing banks until suddenly he realized there was no end to it but a rope. And he had quit, sold a little place he'd owned for years, and started this store in a strange town where nobody knew him. And it had gone well. He had tended to business and stayed out of local fights and politics.

"Maybe I am too late," Canavan said, "but it seems to me a man might find a place on the sidelines and watch for the right moment and then move in.

"You see, I know how Pogue got his ranch. Vin Carter was a friend of mine and Emmett Chubb killed him. He had told me how Pogue forced his old man off his range and took over. Well, I happen to know that none of this range is legally held. It's been preempted, which gives them a claim of sorts. Well, I've a few ideas of my own. And I'm moving in."

"Son," Scott leaned across the table, "listen to me. Pogue's the sort of man to hire killers by the hundred if he needs them. He did force Carter off his range. He took it by force and he has held it by force, and now he wants the whole Valley. So does Reynolds. The Venables are the joker in the deck. Reynolds and Pogue want the Venable place because in a way it is the key to the whole set-up . . . It has the best water and some of the best pasture, but both of them are taking the Venables too lightly. It seems to me they have something up their sleeve . . . or somebody has."

"What do you mean?"

"Well, there's Star Levitt for one. He's no soft touch, that one! And he has some riders who seem to do more work for him than for the Venable outfit—and not all of it honest work."

"Levitt a western man?"

"Could be . . . probably is. Whoever he is, he knows his way around. He's a careful man and to my notion, and I've seen a lot of them, he's a dangerous man. He's the one you've got to watch in this deal, not Pogue or Reynolds!"

Bill Canavan leaned back in his chair. "Those eggs sure tasted good! First I've had in six, maybe seven months. You know how it is in cattle country, all beef and beans."

"That's why I've got them chickens," Scott said. "I told myself someday I'd have chickens and all the eggs I wanted, and I surely have them now."

Scott took up the pot and refilled their cups. "There's something to think on, son. Most folks set their sights too high. They demand too much of life. How many meals can you eat? How many horses can you ride? How many roofs do you have to sleep under? Let me tell you, son, the happy man is the man who is content with just what he needs . . . just so he has it regular.

"Now you take me. I've got this store. I do a fair business. I live in the back of it and I've got a couple of acres of vegetables growing out back. I got me more than a hundred hens, layin' eggs like crazy.

"Down at the edge of town I've got me a friendly Mexican who raises some pigs for me. He tends them, he keeps half, I get half.

"I eat when I feel like it, I do a little business, I set on the porch in the shade time to time, or maybe take a walk down the street and talk with my friends. I no longer have to look over my shoulder for fear some lawman is coming up on me, or maybe some member of my own gang is planning to shoot me to have my share.

"What more do I want? Or need? I ain't eatin' the dust of a trail herd. I ain't rollin' out in the midst of the night to ride around any pesky longhorns, and I don't have to keep an eye out for the law.

"When I want side-meat, I have it. When I want eggs, I eat all I want. I go to sleep at night and I rest easy, and boy, you can do it, too! Take my advice and forget all these wild ideas. You don't stand a chance."

Canavan sipped his coffee. "You may be right, and I probably am a fool for not listening, but this is something I have to do. The trouble is . . . there's a hitch. I need some money. I need a war chest."

Scott put down his cup with a bang. "Well, I'll be damned! You come into this country all primed for trouble, all alone, but with no money! I'll say this for you! You've got nerve. I only hope you've got the gun savvy and the brains you'll need to back it up."

The blue eyes squinted from the leathery face, and he smiled. He was beginning to like Bill Canavan. The nerve of the man appealed to him, and the project was one requiring imagination as well as daring.

"How much do you want?"

"A hundred dollars."

"That all? You won't get far in this country on that."

"All I need is eating money, but along with it I want some advice."

He took a thin leather wallet from inside his coat, and from it he took a beautifully tanned piece of buckskin. Moving the dishes aside, he spread it out on the table. It was a map.

Scott glanced at the map, then leaned forward, suddenly intent. It was drawn to scale and in amazing detail, showing every ranch, line-camp and water-hole. Each stand of trees, each canyon or arroyo was clearly marked along with straight-line distances from one point to another, heights of land and depths of canyons. He could find nothing that was missed.

When Scott sat back in his chair, his expression was mingled respect and worry. "Son, where did you get that map?"

"Made it. Drew it myself. For three years I've talked to every cowhand or sheepherder who ever worked this country. Each one added something, and each one checked what the others had given me. You know how western men are, and most of them can describe a piece of country so you can find your way through it even if you've never been there yourself.

"As a matter of fact, I've had this country in mind for some time. When I was a youngster I knew an old buffalo hunter who trapped in these hills before he turned to killing buffalo for a living. I learned a lot from him. Then the last two or three years I've been picking up a little here, little there. I actually punched cows for a couple of outfits just because they had hands working for them who worked this country in the past.

"Then I ran into Vin Carter, who was born here, and he told me more than all the others. Then, while I was working in a different part of the country, Emmett Chubb rode in and killed the kid . . . picked a fight and shot him down. I think Walt Pogue paid him to do it.

"Sure, I want some range of my own, but that's not all anymore. Vin Carter and me, we rode rough country together. He swam some rivers, fought sandstorms and stampedes, and he was a good man, too good to be murdered by the likes of Chubb.

"Before this is over there's going to be a lot of changes, and before those changes end, I'll be sitting on a nice ranch. Then I'll get married and settle down."

Scott shook his head in amazement. "Kid, you sure do beat all! If I was twenty years younger I'd throw in with you! It's a big order, but I got an idea you're going to give it a try! You can have the hundred dollars."

"And maybe some ammunition, time to time?"

"Sure. But you'll need more than that. You've got to have a plan."

Canavan nodded agreement. "I have one, Scott, and I've already started my action. I've filed on Thousand Springs."

Scott came off his chair, his face a mask of incredulity. "You did *what?*"

"I filed a claim and I've staked her out and started to prove up." Bill Canavan chuckled at Scott's amazement. "Seemed like a good idea to sort of set 'em back on their heels to start. No use wastin' around."

"You've committed suicide," Scott said. "The Thousand Springs is right in the middle of Reynolds's best range. That water-hole is worth a fortune all by itself! That's what this fight is all about!"

"I know it," Canavan said. "I knew it before I took a step. I made my map, studied the country, and studied all I knew about the Valley country. When I heard about Thousand Springs the first thing I did was check into the title. I found it was government land, so I filed a claim. Then I bought Bullhorn."

This time, astonishment was beyond the storekeeper. "How could you buy it? Ain't that government land?"

"No, it isn't, and even Vin Carter believed it was. I checked it out and found the ownership was with a Mexican who'd had it from a Mexican land grant. Finally located him down in the Big Bend country and bought the three hundred acres, the Bullhorn headquarters, the water-hole and the cliffs behind it. And the place includes a fair chunk of the land where Pogue cuts his meadow hay."

"Well, I'll be forever damned!" Scott tapped out his pipe bowl on the hearth. "But what about Hitson Spring?"

"That's another reason why I wanted to see you," Canavan said quietly. "You own it."

"I do, do I? And how'd you come to think that?"

"Met an old sidewinder named Emmons. That was down Laredo way. He was pretty drunk one night down in a greasers' joint. I got him talking about this country and he had a lot to say, an' most of it made sense. Then he told me how foolish you had been to file a claim on that land when you could have bought it from the Indians for little or nothing."

Scott chuckled. "Just what I did, but nobody around here knows that."

"Then sell it to me. I'll give you my note for five thousand right now."

"Your note, is it? Son, you'd better get yourself killed. It will be cheaper to bury you than to pay up." He tapped his pipe bowl out on the hearth again. "Tell you what I'll do. I'll take your note for five hundred and the fun of watching what happens."

Bill Canavan pulled over a tablet that lay on the table and on the first page he wrote out a note and handed it to Scott. The old outlaw chuckled as he read it.

I hereby agree to pay on or before the 15th of March, 1877 to Westbrook Scott, the sum of five hundred dollars and the fun of watching what happens for the 160 acres known as Hitson Spring.

"All right, son! Sign her up! I'll get the deed, and the best of luck to you . . . You'll need it."

Chapter III

When Bill Canavan had pocketed the two deeds, the old man refilled their cups. "Know what you've done? You've laid claim on the three best sources of water in the Valley, the only three that are sure-fire all year around. And what will they do when they find out? They'll kill you, that's what."

"Maybe they won't find out for a while. I don't plan on telling them until matters settle down a mite. Anyway, it's a wonder one of them didn't think of it on his own. They're all so busy trying to take land from one another."

"What about your claim stakes at Thousand Springs?"

"Buried. Iron stakes driven deep into the ground. There's sod and grass over them."

"What about proving up?"

"You know how that spring operates? Actually, there's one great big spring back inside the mountain

20

flowing out through the rocky face of the cliff in hundreds of tiny rivulets. Up atop that mesa there's a good stretch of land that falls into my claim, and back in the woods there was some land I could plow. I've broken that land, smoothed her out and I've put in a crop. I've got a trail to the top of the mesa and I've built a stone house up there. I'm in business, Scotty!"

Scott shook his head, unbelievingly. "I'll say this for you, Canavan. You've got nerve." He got up from the table and went into the store, and when he returned he had several boxes of .44's. "You'd best take those now, but when you come around in the morning you can stock up, grub and whatever you need."

"I'll do it. Meanwhile, you keep track of what I owe and I'll settle every cent before this is over."

"Better make a cache or two," Scott suggested, "hide out an extra gun and some ammunition. Maybe a blanket and some grub. Some place you can get to without trouble. Once they find out what you've done, you'll be on the run."

With money in his pocket Bill Canavan returned to the street. For a moment he stood in the shadows to see if he was observed, but as far as he could see the street was empty and there was no one watching. He stepped out on the street and crossed to the Bit and Bridle.

The bartender glanced at him, then put a bottle on the bar in front of him, and a glass. He was a short man who looked fat, but after noticing the corded forearms, bulging with muscle, Canavan decided little of it could be fat.

A couple of cowhands down the bar were talking lazily, and there was a poker game in progress at a table. Several other men sat around at tables or at benches along the wall. It was the usual crowd to be found in any cattle country saloon.

He had poured his drink and was holding it between his thumb and forefinger when the bat-wing doors behind him opened and he heard a click of heels on the floor. He knew no one here and was expecting no one, so he neither turned nor looked around. He regarded the drink for a moment, then tossed it off. He had never been what might be called a drinking man, and did not intend to drink much tonight.

The footsteps halted behind him, and a quick, clipped voice asked, "Are you the chap who owns that fast Appaloosa?"

He turned half around. There was no need to guess that this was Tom Venable. He was a tall, well set-up young man who was like his sister, with that imperious lift to his chin, but unlike her in his quick, decisive manner.

"I own an Appaloosa," Canavan said. "Some folks think him fast."

"My sister is outside. She wants to speak to you."

"I don't want to speak to her. You can tell her that." He glanced at the bottle, wondering if he wanted another drink.

What happened then happened so fast it caught him off balance. A hard hand grasped him by the shoulder and spun him around in a grip of iron, and he was startled by the strength in that slim hand. Tom Venable's eyes were hot with anger.

"I *said*, my sister wants to speak to you!"

"And I said I did not want to speak to her." Bill Canavan spoke slowly, evenly. "Now take your hand off me, and don't ever lay a hand on me again!"

Tom Venable had never backed down for any man. From the east, he had come west to the cow country. He had made a place for himself by drive, energy, decision and his own youthful strength. Yet suddenly he realized he had never met such a man as the one he faced now. As he met Canavan's level gaze, he felt something turn over inside him. It was as though he had parted the brush and looked into the eyes of a lion.

He dropped his hand. "I'm sorry. My sister can't come into a place like this."

The two men measured each other, and the suddenly alert audience in the Bit and Bridle let their eyes go from Tom Venable to the stranger. Tom they knew well enough to know he was afraid of nothing that walked. They also knew his normal manner was polite to a degree rarely encountered in the west, where manners were apt to be brusque and friendly, but lacking in formality. Yet something else was happening now. There was something intangible between these two, and the men sensed the sudden hesitation in Venable, a wariness that made them look again, very carefully, at the stranger.

The bat-wing doors parted suddenly, and Dixie Venable stepped into the room.

First, Canavan was aware of shock that such a girl would come into such a place, and secondly of shame that he had been the cause. Then he felt admiration for her courage.

Beautiful in a gray tailored riding outfit, her head lifted proudly, she crossed the room and walked up to Canavan, her face very stiff, her eyes bright.

Bill Canavan was aware that never in his life had he looked into eyes so fine, so filled with feeling. "Sir," and her voice could be heard clearly in the silent room, "I do not know what your name may be, but I have come to pay you your money. Your horse beat Flame today, and beat him fairly. I regret the way I acted, but it was such a shock to have Flame beaten that I behaved very rudely and then allowed you to leave without being paid. You won fairly, and I am very sorry."

She paused only a moment, then added, "However, if you would like to run your horse against Flame again, I'll double the bet!"

"Thank you, Miss Venable," Canavan bowed

slightly, from the hips. "It was only your comment about my horse that made me run him at all. As you no doubt know, horses have feelings, and I couldn't allow you to make a slighting remark about my horse, not right to his face, thataway!"

Her eyes were on his and suddenly they crinkled at the corners and her lips rippled with a little smile.

"Now, if you'll allow me—" He took her arm and escorted her from the room. Inside they heard a burst of applause, and he smiled as he held her stirrup for her. She swung to the saddle, and he looked up at her. "I am sorry you had to go in there, but your brother was kind of abrupt."

"That's quite all right," she said quickly, almost too quickly. "Now our business is complete."

Tom Venable had come out of the saloon. And during their brief exchange he had stood back, listening. Now he, too, mounted and they rode away.

Canavan turned back to the saloon and almost ran into a tall, carefully dressed man who had come up behind him. A man equally as large as Pogue.

Pale blue eyes looked out from a handsome, perfectly cut face of city white. The man was trim, neat and precise, and only the guns at his hips struck a discordant note. A pair of guns that gave every indication of use.

"That," said the tall man gesturing after Dixie Venable, "is a staked claim!"

Bill Canavan was irritated. Men who were bigger than he was always irritated him anyway, if their attitude was aggressive. "It is?" His tone was cutting. "If you think you can stake a claim on any woman, you've got a lot to learn!"

Canavan shoved by him toward the doors of the saloon.

Behind him the voice said, "But that one's staked. You hear me?"

Soledad by night was a thin scattering of lights along the dark river of the street. Music from the tinny piano in the Bit and Bridle drifted along the street and into the darkness beyond, and with it came the lazy voice of someone singing a cow-camp song.

Bill Canavan stood for a few minutes on the edge of the boardwalk, let himself forget all he had been thinking about, and just soaked in the night, the melancholy music, and the softness of the lights on the dusty street. He realized suddenly and with greater clarity than ever before that he was a lonely man, a drifting man with no ties, no sense of belonging to anything. And there had been more than enough of that. He wanted to stop, to settle down, to start grazing his own cows, looking out over his own broad fields. He wanted to go to sleep in the same house every night.

Turning, he walked up the street toward the two-story frame hotel, his mind unable to free itself from the vision that was Dixie Venable.

For the first time, the person who was to share that ranch house he planned for had a face. Until now there had been only a vague Somebody in his mind, no definite features, nothing that could be recognized. Now, after meeting Dixie Venable, he knew there could be but one woman in that house he hoped to build.

He smiled wryly as he thought of such a woman sharing his life. How could he think of such a girl marrying a drifting cowhand? And what would her reaction be when she discovered he was Bill Canavan? Not that the name meant very much, for it did not, except in certain quarters where fighting men gathered. Stories about him had drifted across the country, as such stories did. He had no notoriety as a gunfighter, but he was known as a tough, capable man who had survived much hard fighting.

He was completely aware of the situation in the Valley, for he had taken months to learn all the details before ever entering the country. Once his intentions became known, he would be facing trouble, really serious trouble. Yet at first he doubted if they would worry much about a lone man with ambitions.

Pogue had already sensed enough of what he was to offer him a job, but even Pogue—once it was realized what Canavan had done—would have no choice but to buy him out, run him out or kill him.

Or they could move out themselves, and neither Pogue nor Reynolds was the type of man to back up.

The truth of the matter was, he was already holding the reins, and all their fighting would be so much shadow boxing if he survived.

Land was of no value without water, and he who controlled the water controlled the land. Longhorns could graze a day or two from water, walking in for a drink only occasionally, if water was scarce. The vegetation they ate gave them enough moisture to get along, although they preferred to drink every day or twice a day.

He had no plan to take sides in the fight that was brewing, yet what was he to do about the Venables? Until today they had been but names to him. And now, suddenly, Dixie Venable was no longer just a name, and his feelings were involved.

He stopped in front of the hotel and shook his head like an old bull. He could not afford sentiment. He had planned for no such complication. He would be a free agent, coming in and watching the rivals kill each other off, then stepping in holding all the aces. It had been a good plan. It was still a good plan, if he could just forget Dixie Venable.

Yet even as he considered avoiding her, driving toward his goal with no interest but victory, he knew he would not do it. Just to the degree that he was interested in her, so his strength was weakened. And to win the fight he was in called for complete concentration, and no involvement of feeling with anyone.

His thinking nettled him even as it amused him, for he viewed himself with a kind of wry, ironic humor, seeing himself always with more clarity than others saw him.

Thinking back over the day, he knew he had moved forward a little. He had arrived. He had met Scott and set up a valuable relationship, and he had taken the measure of at least one of the participants in the fight. Also, he had found out that Emmett Chubb was in the country.

That was, perhaps, most important of all. For he would not want Chubb to see him first, and without warning. That small edge might mean the difference.

He had been sure in his own mind that Chubb worked for Pogue, but now it developed that he worked for Reynolds. Had he always been there? Or had he switched sides? Was that why Pogue wanted him killed, a thousand dollars' worth?

His thoughts turned to the Venables. Tom was all man. And whatever Pogue and Reynolds were thinking, Tom Venable would be no soft touch. Easterner he might be, but he was a solid citizen and the sort of man who would get tougher as the situation did.

What of the cowhands who Scott implied were loyal to Levitt rather than Venable? These men must be considered too, for he must be aware of all the conflicting elements in the Valley.

Now he realized who the big man outside the Bit and Bridle had been. Carter had mentioned him, but with some uncertainty for he was new in the Valley then and an unknown quantity. But the man who claimed to have staked a claim on Dixie Venable was Star Levitt.

With that instinctive awareness an experienced man has for such things, Bill Canavan knew there

Chapter IV

The hotel was a long building of thirty-odd rooms, a large but empty lobby with a buffalo's head on the wall behind the desk, a couple of leather settees and several leather chairs. Adjoining the lobby was a restaurant, and feeling like another cup of coffee, his eyes went to the restaurant. Then he walked up to the desk.

He dropped his war-bag, and a young man standing in an inner doorway walked to the desk and turned the register around. "Room?" His was a pleasant smile.

"The best you've got," Canavan said, smiling back.

The clerk shrugged. "Sorry, but they are all equally bad, although reasonably clean. Take fifteen, at the end of the hall. You'll be closer to the well."

"Pump?"

"What do you think this is? New York? It's a rope and bucket well but it's been almost a year since we hauled the dead man out. The water should be pure enough by now."

"Depends on who he was," Canavan said. He gave the clerk a thoughtful look. "Where you from, New York?"

"New York, Philadelphia, Boston, Richmond and London . . . and now, Soledad."

"You've been around." Canavan signed his name. "How's the food?"

"Good. Very good, in fact, and the prettiest waitress west of the Mississippi."

"Yeah? And if she's like the other girls around here she's probably a staked claim. I had a big gent with a white hat inform me tonight that at least one girl was a staked claim, and to lay off."

The clerk gave him a quick, shrewd glance. "Star Levitt?"

"I figured so."

"If he meant the lady you had the race with today, I'd say he was doing more hoping than otherwise. Dixie Venable is not an easy claim to stake."

The clerk turned the register around and looked at the signature. *Bill Canavan, El Paso.*

He held out his hand. "Glad to meet you, Bill. My name's Allen Kinney." He glanced at the name again. "Bill Canavan . . . now I've heard that name somewhere.

"It's funny about names and towns. Canavan from El Paso. Now you might be from Del Rio or Eagle Pass or Laredo. You might have come from Uvalde or Deadwood or Cheyenne.

"What happened in El Paso? Or wherever you come from? Men drift without reason sometimes, but usually there is a reason—a woman, gun trouble, or whatever. Sometimes the law is behind them, or an outlaw just a jump or two ahead of them. Occasionally, of course, men move just to be moving, just for a change of scene. But you, now, I'd say you had a reason to come to Soledad."

"Let's drink some coffee," Canavan invited. "And I'll see if that waitress is as pretty as you say."

"You won't think so," Kinney said, shaking his head, "you won't think so at all. You've just seen Dixie Venable. After her, all women seem washed out . . . until you get over her."

"I don't plan on it."

Kinney led the way into the restaurant and dropped into a chair. "That, my friend, is a large order. Miss Venable usually handles such situations with neatness and dispatch. She is always pleasant, never familiar."

"This is different." Canavan looked up. And with a sudden excitement, he knew what he was going to say, knew he should not say it, but said it nonetheless. "I'm going to marry her."

Allen Kinney smiled tolerantly. "Have you told her? Does she know your intentions are honorable? Does she even know you have intentions?" He shook his head, amused but thoughtful. "That's no small task you have laid out for yourself."

The waitress came to their table with a coffee pot. She was a slender, very pretty girl with red hair, a few freckles and a certain bubbling good humor that was infectious.

"May," Kinney said, "I want you to meet Mr. Bill Canavan. He says he is going to marry Dixie Venable."

Canavan felt his ears growing red, and he cursed himself for a fool for ever saying such a thing in the first place. It had been startled from him by the sudden realization that he intended to do just that.

"What?" May was startled. "Another one?"

Bill Canavan looked up and put his hand over hers. "No, May. *The* one."

Their eyes held for an instant and her laughter faded. "You know," she said seriously, "you just might!"

She took their orders and left. Kinney shook his

head thoughtfully. "You have made an impression. I think May believed you. Now if you can do as well with Miss Venable, you'll be on your way."

The street door opened and two men came into the room. One of the men was big, with sloping shoulders. And as he caught sight of Canavan his eyes narrowed as if with recognition. The other man was shorter, thicker, but obviously a hard-case. With a queer sort of premonition Canavan guessed these men were from the Venable ranch—riders who already knew of Bill Canavan's presence and were more than casually interested.

These could be men working for Star Levitt, and as such they merited study. Yet their type was familiar to anyone who rode the wild country. Many a cowhand has slapped a brand on a maverick when he needed a little drinking money, but these were men who rode the outlaw trail.

These were men who rode with their guns for hire. But they were not simply warriors who fought as did the clansmen of Scotland for their lairds, or for the men who paid their wages. These were men who were ready for crooked money of any kind. He had known such men before, faced their kind in many places, and he knew they recognized him for what he was. These were not feudal retainers. But men never fought a battle but for themselves or the hope of gain.

They had scarcely seated themselves when the door opened a second time, shoved hard this time, and two more men entered. The first was a short, stocky man who walked with a peculiar, jerky lift to his knees. He walked now, right over to Canavan.

"You're Bill Canavan?" he said abruptly. "I've got a job for you! You start tomorrow morning! Hundred a month an' food! Plenty of horses! I'm Charlie Reynolds of the CR, and my place is just outside of town in that big grove of cottonwoods. Old place. You won't have any trouble finding it." He pulled a roll of bills from his pocket. "Need any money now?"

"Sorry, I'm not looking for a job."

"What's that? Not looking for a job? At a hundred a month? When the average range-hand is makin' thirty?"

"I said I didn't want a job."

"Ah?" The genial light had gone from his eyes, leaving them mean and cruel. "So that's it! You've gone to work for Pogue!"

"No, I don't work for Pogue. I don't work for any man. I ride my own trails."

Reynolds stared hard at him, and Canavan guessed he was a man who expected to be feared. "Listen, my friend, and listen well. In these hills and in this valley there are two sides, and only two sides, those *for* Reynolds and those against him. If you do not work for me, I shall regard you as an enemy!"

Canavan shrugged. "That's your funeral, Reynolds, but from all I hear you've enough enemies without making any more. Also, from what I hear you deserve them."

"*What?*" Reynolds had turned away but now he took a step back. "Don't sass me, Canavan!"

The lean, whip-bodied man beside him interfered. "Let me handle this, Uncle Charlie," he said gently. "Let me talk to this man."

Canavan shifted his attention. The younger man had a lantern jaw and unusually long gray eyes. The eyes had a flatness to them that puzzled and warned him.

"My name is Sydney Berdue. I am foreman for Mr. Reynolds." He stepped closer to where Canavan sat in his chair. "Maybe you'd like to tell me why he deserves his enemies."

Canavan's blunt features were innocent of expression, his eyes faintly curious but steady and aware. "Sure, I'd be glad to," he said, "if Mr. Reynolds wishes."

"You're talkin'. Now tell us."

"Charlie Reynolds came west from Missouri right

after the war with Mexico. He located in Santa Fe for a while, but when the wagon trains started along the Overland Trail he went north and began selling guns to the Indians."

Reynolds's face went white, then flushed with anger. "That's not true!"

Canavan's words were sharp. "Don't make me kill you, Reynolds, although you damned well deserve it! Every word I say is true and can be documented. You yourself took part in wagon-train raids, and you collected your share of the white scalps. You got out of there with a good deal of loot, and met a man in Julesburg who wanted to come out here and go to ranching. He knew nothing of your crooked background—"

Berdue went for his gun, but Canavan was expecting it. When the Reynolds foreman stepped closer, he had come beyond Canavan's outstretched feet. Canavan hooked a toe behind Berdue's ankle, jerked hard and at the same moment stiff-armed him with an open hand.

Berdue hit the floor with a crash and his gun went off into the ceiling. From the room overhead there was a startled shout and a sound of bare feet hitting the floor.

Canavan kicked the gun from Berdue's hand, then swept it up.

"Get up, Berdue! Reynolds, get over there against the wall! You, too, Berdue!"

White-faced, hatred burning in his eyes, Reynolds backed to the wall. Behind him the room was slowly filling with onlookers. "Now," Canavan said, "I'll finish what I started. And remember, you asked for it.

"You asked why I thought you deserved your enemies. I started by telling about the people you murdered along the wagon trails, and the money you made from selling guns to the Indians. And now I'll tell you about the man you met in Julesburg."

Reynolds's face was ashen. "Forget that. You're talkin' too much. Berdue was huntin' trouble and he got it. You just forget it. I need a good man and I'll pay good money."

"To murder somebody like you did your partner? You made a deal with him and he came down here and worked hard. He planted those trees, he built that house. Then three of you went out and stumbled into a band of Indians and somehow, although wounded, you were the only one who got back. Naturally, the ranch was all yours.

"Who were those Indians, Reynolds? Or was there only *one* Indian? The last man of three riding single-file?

"You wanted to know why I wouldn't work for you and why you should have enemies, and I've told you. Now I'll tell you something else. I've come to the Valley to stay. I am not leaving."

Deliberately then, he handed the gun back to Berdue, who took the gun, reversed it and started it into its holster. Then his hand stopped and his lips tightened.

Bill Canavan seemed to be smiling. "Careful, Berdue! I wouldn't try it, if I were you."

Berdue hesitated. Then with an oath he shoved the gun down hard into the holster and, turning, walked rapidly out of the room. Behind him went Charlie Reynolds, his neck and ears red with the bitterness of the fury that throbbed in his veins.

Slowly, in a babble of talk, the room cleared, and Bill Canavan sat down again. "May," he said, "you've let my coffee get cold. Fill it up, will you?"

Chapter V

Those who lived in the town of Soledad and the surrounding country were not unaccustomed to sensation. But the calling of Reynolds and his supposedly gun-handy foreman in the Cattleman's Café was a subject that had the old maids of both sexes licking their lips with excitement. Nor was the subject ignored by others. And, the west being what it was, the news traveled.

Little had been known of the background of the man who called himself Charlie Reynolds. And being what it was, the west did not ask questions. It was up to every man to prove himself and to show what manner of man he was.

Reynolds was the oldest settler, the owner of the largest and oldest ranching operation, and he was known as a hard character when pushed. Yet now they were viewing him in a new light, and nobody liked what they had heard.

Not the last to hear was Walt Pogue, who chuckled and slapped his thigh. "Wouldn't you know it? The old four-flusher! Crooked as a dog's hind leg!"

The next thing that occurred to anyone occurred to him. How had Bill Canavan known? And what else did he know?

That thought brought Pogue up short, and all his satisfaction at the discomfiture of Reynolds vanished. This man Canavan knew too much . . . Who was he, anyway? And what did he want here? If Canavan knew that, he might . . . no, that did not necessarily follow. Still, Bill Canavan would be a good man to have for a friend, and a bad enemy.

Not the least of the comment had revolved around Canavan's confidence, the way he had stood and dared Berdue to draw. Overnight Canavan had become the most talked-about man in that part of the country.

When gathering his information about the Valley country, Bill Canavan had gleaned other information that was of the greatest interest, and that information was very much on his mind when he got out of bed the following morning.

So far he had no opportunity to verify this last fragment of information, but now he intended to do just that. From what he overheard and what he had learned before coming to this part of the country, the area north and west of the mountains was a badlands avoided by all. It was lava-flow country, broken and jagged, with much evidence of prehistoric volcanic action. Riding there was a danger, and walking was a sure way to ruin a good pair of boots.

At one time there had been a man who knew the lava beds and all that part of the country that occupied some three hundred square miles. That man had been Jim Burge.

It had been Jim Burge who had told Charlie Hastings, Reynolds's ill-fated partner, about the Valley country. And it had been Jim Burge who drove the first herd of Spanish cattle into the Valley. Burge tired of ranching, his itching foot getting the best of him, and he headed north, leaving his ranch and letting his cattle go where they willed. He had taken with him only a few of his best horses.

He had talked to Charlie Hastings, and Hastings had repeated the story to Reynolds, but by that time, Burge was gone. Gone into the Texas Panhandle, and a lone fight with Comanches that ended only when four Comanches were dead and the fifth tied Burge's scalp to his horse's bridle.

Jim Burge had talked to other people in Santa Fe, and those people did not forget, either. One of those was Bill Canavan. And Bill was a curious man.

When he threw his saddle on the Appaloosa, he had decided to satisfy that curiosity before matters went any further. He was going to find out what had become of those cattle.

Nine years had passed since Burge had left them to shift for themselves, and in nine years several hundred head of cattle can do pretty well for themselves.

"There's water in those badlands if you know where to find it," Burge had assured him. "And there's grass, if you know where to look." Knowing range cattle, Canavan was not worried about them finding either water or grass, and if he could find it he could find them . . . unless somebody else had.

So he rode out of Soledad along the main trail, and a number of curious eyes watched him go. One pair of those eyes belonged to Dixie Venable, inspecting her cattle and seeing where and how they fared. She noted the tall rider on the oddly marked horse . . . and felt a queer tug at her heart at the thought that he was riding away, perhaps forever.

Yet, remembering the way he had looked at her and the hard set to his jaw, she doubted he would be leaving for good. Such a man would surely return . . . Wouldn't he?

The story of his meeting with Reynolds and Berdue had come to her ears among the first. Berdue had always frightened her, for whenever they were near, his eyes were always upon her. They gave her a crawling sensation not at all like the excitement she drew from the quick, amused eyes of Bill Canavan.

She found herself thinking more and more of Canavan. The cool hardness of him masked gentleness and consideration, she was sure, yet he had a temper, and his manner of handling Reynolds had been rough, really rough. A foolish action, some might say, making an enemy of a dangerous man when it was unnecessary . . . But was that true? How could she say without knowing more about Bill Canavan?

The Appaloosa was a good horse for rough country, and now he went quickly forward, ears pricked, eyes alert. These were the sights and smells he knew best, for he had run wild upon the range nearly four years before being captured and broken by Canavan.

Whether he wanted it that way or not, Canavan knew he was now in the very center of things, with all eyes upon him. From now on he must move swiftly and with boldness, but it would be helpful to keep them guessing just a little longer. Things were due to break wide open between Pogue and Reynolds, especially now that his own needling of Reynolds might stir the man into aggressive action.

Reynolds was no fool. He would know how fast the talk would spread, and it might not be long before embarrassing questions might be asked. The only escape from those questions lay in power. He must move quickly to put himself beyond questions. Eyes squinted against the glare, Canavan tried to think what Reynolds might do. It was his move, and Canavan had no doubt he would strike. But where? How?

The trail he sought showed itself suddenly, just a faint track off through the piñons, and he turned into it, letting the Appaloosa choose his own gait.

It was mid-afternoon before Canavan reached the edge of the lava beds. The black tumbled masses seemed without trails and only the sparsest vegetation. He skirted the end of the lava flow where broken blocks had tumbled down along the face of the flow, searching for some indication of a trail. It was miserably hot and the sun threw back heat from the rocks until he felt like he was living in an oven. When he was on a direct line between Thousand Springs and the lava beds, he rode up the slope of a nearby mountain until he found an area of shade. And there he swung down to give his horse a rest. While the Appaloosa cropped casually at the dry grass, he got out a set of field glasses he had purchased in New Orleans a year earlier. Then he began a systematic search, inch by inch, of the lava beds.

As yet he had but the vaguest of plans. But if the cattle he sought were there, he hoped to brand them and slip them out into the Valley, using that method to make his own bid for Valley range.

From previous experience, he knew that such lava beds often had islands of grass in their midst, places where the flow had been diverted by some obstruction and the lava had flowed around, walling in patches of pasture sometimes of considerable extent. Ice caves were not infrequent. And often there were long tunnels where the outer surface of the lava had hardened, while molten rock continued to flow beneath the hard outer shell until it had passed on, leaving a natural tunnel. Some he had known were several hundred yards long, and he had heard of one that was several miles in extent.

To look at the lava beds, they seemed barren but empty, and to the casual passerby, a place without mystery or attraction. The end of the flow was abrupt, a wall some fifteen to twenty feet high. Beyond it the surface looked ropey, in some places like great masses of congealed molasses. After a half hour of study, he remounted Rio and walked the horse slowly along the side of the hill, pausing from time to time to renew his study of the lava beds.

It was almost dusk when he pointed the glass toward a tall finger of rock that thrust itself upward from the beds. At the base of the rock was a cow. And as he watched, she slowly began to drift off toward the northwest.

Try as he might he could find no trail into the beds, so as dusk was near he started back toward Thousand Springs. He would try again. At least he knew there was one cow in that labyrinth. And if there was one, there would almost certainly be more.

The trail he had chosen led him up the mesa above Thousand Springs by a little-known route. He wound around through clumps of piñon until he topped out on the relatively flat surface. After that he rode slowly, drinking in the beauty of the place he had chosen for his home. Purple haze had thickened over the distant hills and gathered shadows around the trees in the forested notches. The pines fringed the sky with blackness, and a star appeared. Then another.

Below him the mesa broke sharply off and fell for over a hundred feet of sheer rock. Thirty feet from the bottom of the cliff, the springs for which the place was named trickled from the fractured rock, covering the rock with a silver sheen of water from which many small cascades fell into the pool below.

Beyond the pool's far edge, fringed with aspens, the Valley swept away in a long sweep of grassy range rolling into the dark distance against the mystery of the far-off hills. Bill Canavan sat his horse in a place rarely visited by men, for he doubted if anyone had climbed to the mesa's top since the last Indian had done so. At least, he had found no tracks nor sign nor horse, no cow nor man, and nothing but the fallen ruins of an ancient stone house—or houses—that seemed to have no connection with any of the cliff dwellings or pueblos he had seen.

The range below him was the upper Valley, supposedly controlled by Charlie Reynolds. Actually, he
rarely visited the place, nor did any of his riders. It
was far away from any of Reynolds's other holdings,
yet the water below was available to cattle when
they wished to come to it, as did the deer, antelope
and wild horses.

Just back from the rim in a grove of piñon was
where Canavan had started to build his house, using
a foundation laid by the prehistoric builders—part of
their floor, and many of their stones. The floor
covered a wider expanse than he planned for his first
house, so he swept it clean, paced it off, and planned
what he would do. For the moment he was intent
only on rebuilding a part of the old house to use as his
claim shanty.

There was water here, bubbling up from the same
source as Thousand Springs. He knew the water came
from the same source, because several times he had
dropped sticks into the spring only to have them appear in the pool, far below.

From where he sat he could with his glass watch
several miles of trail and see all who approached
him. The trail up the back way was unknown so far
as he had been able to discover, and the only tracks
he had found were those of wild game.

To the east and south his view was unobstructed.
Below him lay all the dark distance of the Valley and
the range for which he was fighting. On the north the
mesa fell sheer away into a deep canyon with a dry
wash at the bottom. The opposite side of the canyon
was nearly as sheer as this, and almost a quarter of a
mile away.

The trail led up from the west and through a
broken country of tumbled rock, long fingers of lava,
and clumps of piñon giving way to aspen and pine.
The top of the mesa was at least two hundred acres
in extent and impossible to reach by any other route
but that he had used.

Returning through the trees to a secluded hollow, he swung down and stripped the gear from the Appaloosa and turned it loose. He rarely hobbled or tied the horse, for Rio would come to him at his call or whistle and never failed to respond at once. A horse in most cases will not wander far from a camp fire, feeding away from it, then feeding back toward it, seeming to like the sense of comfort a camp fire offered as much as a man.

He built his fire of dry wood, keeping it small. Down in the hollow as he was, there was no danger of it being seen and causing wonder. The last thing he wanted now was for anyone in the Valley to find him out.

After he had eaten, he strolled back to the open ground where the house was taking shape. Part of the ancient floor he was keeping as a sort of terrace from which to view the Valley below.

For a long time he stood, looking off into the darkness and enjoying the cool night air. Then he turned and walked back into the deep shadows where the house stood. He was standing there, considering the work yet to be done, when he heard a low, distant rumble.

Suddenly anxious, he stood very still, listening. The sound seemed to come from the very rock on which he stood. He waited, expecting the sound to grow. But after only a minute or so it died away to a vague muttering, then it ceased. Puzzled, he walked around for several minutes, waiting and listening, but there was no further sound.

It was a strange thing, and it left him disturbed and uneasy as he walked back to his camp. Long after he lay in his blankets he puzzled over the sound. He had been a boy of five in California when the greatest earthquake in Southern California history hit in 1857. This had not felt like an earthquake, yet it was something deep underground.

He noted with an odd sense of disquiet that Rio

stayed close to him, closer than usual. Of course, there could be another reason for that. There were cougars on the mesa and in the breaks behind it. He had seen their tracks, as he had seen those of elk, deer, and even bear.

The country in which he had chosen to settle was wildly beautiful—a strange, lost corner of the land cut off by the rampart of Thousand Springs Mesa.

He awakened with the sky growing gray, and found himself sitting bolt upright. And then he heard it again, that low mounting rumble, far down in the rock beneath him—as though the very spirit of the mountain was beneath him in his sleep. Only here the sound was less plain. It was fainter, farther away.

"It's all right, Rio," he spoke quietly. "It's all right."

And he hoped it was. . . .

Chapter VI

When he awakened again the sky was
light. He rolled out of his bed, started a small fire and
put on the water for coffee. While eating, he puzzled
over the strange sounds of the previous night. The
only logical solution seemed to be that the sounds
came from the springs, from forces of some kind that
were at work deep under the mesa.

Obviously these forces had made no recent changes in the contour of the rock itself. So they must be
insufficient for the purpose, and probably of no im-
mediate danger. When he had finished breakfast, he
packed up and made ready to travel. Only then did
he return to work on the house.

Unlike many cowhands, who preferred to do no
work that could not be done from the back of a horse,
Canavan had always enjoyed working with his hands.
Now he had the double pleasure of knowing that
what he built he built for himself. By noon he had

completed another wall of heavy stone, and his house was beginning to take shape.

He stopped briefly to eat and slipped on his shirt before sitting down. As he buttoned it he caught a faint movement from far down the Soledad trail. Digging out the field glass, he took a position on the rim-rock. And making sure the flash of sunlight from his glass would not give him away, he studied the approaching rider.

Canavan was too far to be sure of his identity, but there was something familiar about the rider. And only when he drew nearer was Canavan sure. It was Sydney Berdue.

What was the Reynolds foreman doing out here? Of course, as this was CR range he might just be checking the water or the stock. Yet he was riding at a good pace and taking no time to notice anything around him. When he reached the pool down below, he swung down, seated himself on a rock and lit a cigarette.

Waiting for someone!

The sun was warm and comfortable after the hard work of the morning, and Canavan settled himself down to wait. If Berdue was meeting somebody out here, he wanted to know who it was. Several times he turned his glass down the trail, but saw nothing. Yet when he swept the glass to cover the country around, he found another rider—a man on a sorrel with three white stockings, who must have come up through the timber, as he was not in sight until the very last minute. He rode up to the pool and stepped down from the saddle. Puzzled, Canavan shifted his glass to the brand.

The sorrel wore a VV on his shoulder! A Venable rider meeting Berdue of the CR at what was apparently a secret meeting place. Now he saw two more riders approaching, and one of them was the big, slope-shouldered man he had seen in the restaurant, and he rode a Box N horse. The last man rode a gray mustang, wearing Star Levitt's Three Diamonds on his hip!

Now this was something to think about. A secret meeting of men representing four brands, two of them outwardly at war and the others on the verge of it. Canavan cursed his luck that he could not hear what was said. But from where he watched it looked like Berdue was laying down the law. He was doing the talking, with emphatic gestures, pacing up and down as he spoke.

Then Canavan saw something else.

At first it was only a vague suggestion of movement in the grass and brush near the foot of the cliff. And then he glimpsed a slight figure, edging nearer to the talking men. His heart chilled as he saw that it was Dixie Venable, creeping ever closer!

Whatever the meeting of the four might mean, it certainly was obvious they did not wish to be seen or heard, and if Dixie were seen she would be in great danger. Pulling back from the cliff's edge, he ran to the place where he had been working and caught up his rifle. By the time he got back into position, the meeting was breaking up, and whatever they had meant to decide was now decided. One by one the men mounted and rode away. Sydney Berdue was the last to go.

The girl lay very still below him, and only after they had been gone for several minutes did she rise and walk down to the spring for a drink. She drank, then stood as if in profound thought. Finally, she drank again then went into the brush. Shortly afterward, she emerged on Flame.

She was no more than two hundred yards away. But by the time Canavan could have got his horse and ridden around there, nearly an hour would be gone, and so would she.

He lay still and watched her ride away. What had she heard? And what had aroused her suspicions of double-dealing? There had been a meeting here of men from the four brands, but not of the leaders. And she must have had some intimation that such a meeting was to take place or she could not have followed so carefully.

Moreover, she had moved along that hill like an Indian. Not one of the men below was what you would call a tenderfoot, yet she had approached them and listened without giving herself away. Dixie Venable, he decided, would bear watching.

It was time he returned to Soledad. That he might be riding into trouble, he was ready to believe. But he had expected trouble when he first rode into the Valley. It was one eventuality for which he had been prepared. He had not been prepared for Dixie.

Mentally and physically he had prepared himself for what was to come. He had gathered the intelligence necessary, and understood the chances he was taking. But he had known for months that a shooting war was about to break loose, and he hoped to be a winner when it was over.

Saddling Rio, he rode back through the aspens and then down the narrow and dangerous trail to the Valley floor. He had found no way to enter the lava beds and, if he was to take the next step in his pattern for conquest, he must find the cattle that he was sure must still roam that remote area.

The afternoon was well along before he found himself skirting the rim of a canyon that opened near the lava flows. And when he reached them, it was already late. There would be little time for a search, but despite that he turned north, planning to cut back around the mesa and return to Soledad by way of the Springs. Movement among the trees brought him up short, and he waited, watching several elk drifting slowly down a small wash toward the lava beds.

Suddenly he held his breath. There was no water of which he knew nearer than Thousand Springs, yet these elk were walking away from it rather than toward it. As they usually watered at sundown or be-

fore daybreak, they must be headed toward some
other source of water, and that could only be in the
lava beds.

He sat his horse and waited while the elk crossed
before him, and when they vanished into the trees, he
followed. He could dimly see their tracks, and they
led him to a narrow cleft between two great folds of
the black rocks, a space scarcely wide enough for his
stirruped feet to pass without scraping the walls, its
entrance concealed by an overlap of one wall.

Riding carefully, for the trail continued narrow
and the walls on either side were black and rough,
he followed the elk. It was easy to see how such a
trail might exist for years and not be found, for at
least once he actually had to draw one leg up and
hold the stirrup in the saddle to pass through a narrow
opening.

The trail wound around and around, covering
much distance without penetrating very far. The rocks
on each side were rarely more than a few feet above
his head when mounted, except occasionally when for
some reason—an obstruction, no doubt—the lava had
piled up even higher. Suddenly the trail dipped down
through a dangerous-looking cleft. For the first time,
he hesitated. If a man were trapped or hurt in this
lava bed he would die here. If any other human being had ever followed this route, he had left no sign of
his passing, although it was likely Indians had, in
some bygone time. Yet by and large Indians avoided
such desolate areas. Lava was hell on moccasins and
rarely would game be found there.

A moment only he hesitated, then with many
an upward glance at the poorly balanced chunks of
rock, many of them weighing tons, he followed the
trail of the elk into the cleft.

He felt his heart pounding. Even the Appaloosa
was wary, taking the trail with great care as they
went down, the horse almost on his haunches. For a
half mile or more the trail wound steadily downward,

and he was soon well below the level of the surrounding country. He rode on, however, despite the gathering darkness—already pitch-black in the closest parts of the cleft. Suddenly the trail opened out and he drew up with a startled gasp.

Before him lay a great circular valley, an enormous valley for such a situation, surrounded by towering black cliffs which in many places shelved out over the edge. The bottom was almost level and covered with rich green grass. There were a few scattered clumps of trees and from somewhere the sound of running water.

He walked his horse out into the meadow, looking up and around. The valley lay far below the rims of the cliffs, and the unending sameness of the view from above safely concealed its existence. It was, without doubt, an ancient volcanic crater, perhaps the very one from which all the lava had flowed. Some such craters were filled with lakes, but this was simply meadow. And the grass was dotted with cattle, most of them in excellent shape. There were also some horses, descendants of those left by Jim Burge.

Despite the growing darkness he pushed on, wondering at the towering walls, the green grass and the slim white trunks of the aspens. The cattle gazed at him curiously, seemingly unafraid.

In a small glade among the aspens, he drew up and stepped down. Stripping the gear from the Appaloosa, he made camp. This would end what supplies he had brought along, and tomorrow he must start back. Yet this would be a place to start such a cache of supplies as Scott had advised.

Night brought coolness to the valley. He built a fire and made coffee, talking to Rio meanwhile. Then he became aware of movement. Looking up he saw himself surrounded, but well back at the edge of the light, by a dozen cows and a bull. They were staring at the fire and at him with amazed bovine eyes. Apparently they had never seen a man before, and more than likely this was their first fire.

From all appearances the crater had been a large one, several miles across and carpeted with rich grass. Twice during the night he heard the cry of a cougar, and once the howl of a wolf.

He gathered wood from under the trees and made a little stack close by the fire. There were many fallen branches, toppled trees, and bits of bark, fuel enough to keep a fire going for the rest of his life. The water was excellent, and there was game. Literally, a man could live here forever . . . and if that passage should be blocked, he might have to.

The thought worried him. He walked out away from the fire, the cattle moving back as he neared them, and looked around at what he could see of the rim.

There was no break that he could see, and it was very likely there was none. A man caught in the bottom of this crater would have to spend his life here unless he was a good enough rock-climber to find a way up the cliffs.

At this altitude there would be snow, and during most of the winter a man would be snowed in. He walked back to his camp feeling distinctly uneasy. He had no desire to be trapped, even in such a beautiful place as this.

With daylight, he was in the saddle once more. But by day the crater seemed smaller than it had the previous night. There were several smaller craters that broke into this one, and while riding about, scouting the area and making a tentative count of the cattle, he saw several ice caves. These were caused, no doubt, by the mass cooling so unevenly that when the surface had become cold and hard the material below was still molten. As the fluid drained away, the caves were formed under the solid crust. Because lava is a poor heat conductor, the cold air of the caves was protected. Ice formed there, no matter how warm it might be on the surface, and here and there pools of water had gathered on the floors. And these had been used as watering places by wild horses, deer, elk, and bighorn sheep.

When at last he started back toward the cleft through which he had gained entrance to the crater, he was sure there were four or five hundred head of cattle in the bottom, too many for the area now. Probably there had been an unusual increase due to natural factors.

Yet when he reached the place where he believed the cleft to be, it was not there. For a moment he sat his horse, studying the cliff, and several minutes later he thought he had it. But it was only when he found his own tracks that he was able to locate the cleft. The landmarks he had chosen at night had proved useless by day.

He started into the cleft, and for part of the distance it proved a scramble for Rio. Yet from time to time Canavan drew up to let the Appaloosa catch his wind. Glancing up at the overhanging rocks, he made a mental note that someday he would climb up there and see just how secure they were.

It was dusk of another day before he cantered into the main street of Soledad and rode up to the livery stable. A Mexican came to the door, glanced at the brand on his horse and then at him.

"Do you ride for Señor Pogue or Señor Reynolds?" he asked, warily.

"Only for myself," Canavan replied. "What's the matter? The town seems too quiet."

"Si, Señor. There has been a keeling. Rolly Burt of the CR was in a shooting with two hands from the Box N. One was killed, one wounded, and Burt, I think, was wounded also. He is gone."

"Left the country?"

"Who knows? He was wounded, they say, and I am sorry for that, for he was a good man, Señor

Burt." The Mexican lighted a smoke and said reflectively, "Perhaps he was no longer wanted on the CR, either."

"Why do you say that?" Canavan asked quickly.

"There had been trouble, much trouble with Señor Berdue. Señor Burt told me himself."

Berdue had trouble with Burt, yet Burt was attacked by two Box N hands? That did not seem to tie in, yet why not? Maybe that was one of the results of the conference at Thousand Springs. In any event, this would start hostilities again.

Rolly Burt was a good man, the Mexican said, and if the Mexican thought so the chances were he was right. This was an area where Mexicans were not always treated well, which hinted that Burt was a friendly man, not apt to take advantage.

He was also good with a gun. Facing two men he killed one and put lead into the other. Not bad . . . not bad at all.

Rolly Burt might be a man he could use.

Chapter VII

Leaving Rio to be cared for, Canavan returned to his room in the Cattlemen's Hotel. Kinney was not in the lobby when he entered, and he found no one on the stairs. He realized how precarious was his own position. Although the house he was building seemed reasonably safe from discovery, there was every chance someone might stumble on the land he had plowed back in the trees. What he had done was not much, but enough to show that somebody was working on the place.

Uneasily, he studied the situation while he changed clothes, bathed and shaved. So far, everything was proceeding according to plan . . . and almost too well. He had his water rights nailed down. He had found the cattle. In the crater and on the mesa he had two bases of action that were reasonably safe from discovery, yet the situation was due to blow wide open at any moment.

Berdue seemed to be playing a deep game, and it might be with the connivance of his uncle, but Canavan found himself doubting it. Perhaps he had the same idea Canavan had, that from the range war would come a new situation where Berdue or someone like him would be in command.

Berdue's part puzzled Canavan, but at least he knew by sight the men Berdue met at the Springs, and he would be able to keep an eye on them. Of course, there were some strangers at the VV, and he wanted to have a look at them. In fact, a visit to the VV seemed much in order.

A dozen or more people were eating in the Cattleman's Café when he entered. He stopped, surveying the various groups with care. He had no desire to run into Berdue or Reynolds unaware, for Berdue would not and Reynolds dared not ignore him. He had stepped into the scene in Soledad in no uncertain terms.

Suddenly, at a small table alone, he spotted Dixie Venable. On impulse he walked over, spurs jingling. She glanced up, momentarily surprised.

"Oh? It's you again! I thought you had left town!"

"After seeing you? How could I?" He indicated the chair opposite her. "May I sit down?"

"Surely." She looked at him thoughtfully. "You know, Mr. Canavan, you're not an unhandsome sort of man, but I've got a feeling you're pretty much of a savage."

"I live in a country that is savage," he replied simply. "No one has ever discovered how to tame a wild land filled with untamed people, both white and red, without some savagery. This is a hard, hard land, and a lovely land, too. But it does not want the weak and the submissive. The land demands the best one can give it, and will settle for nothing less.

"Oddly enough, I feel the land demands honor, too. That may not seem to fit with savagery, but as a matter of fact, it does. The wrong kind of man may seem to win for a time, but never for long . . . The wild country has too many ways of tricking him because of the fatal defects in his character."

"I had no idea you were a moralist," she said ironically.

He shrugged a shoulder. "Call it what you will. I'm not a gospel shouter, just a man who has lived around and watched his fellow man. You find a man who is heedless of others and it will often carry over into other things. And the wild country, the desert and the mountains, leaves one very little margin for survival.

"You ride down a corridor, and as long as you stay within the limits you are safe. But if you get out of line you're in trouble.

"If a man crosses a mountain or a desert, he is well advised to stay on the beaten trail . . . The trail is there because people have found it the right way to go, and if you take another route you may have to come back, or find yourself without water and with no way to get back.

"It is much the same with other things. Because a custom is old is no reason for junking it . . . Men have found it the best way to go, and to deviate too far is to ask for trouble."

"How are you progressing with your invasion?" she asked. "Are you like Alexander, looking for new worlds to conquer? Or have you decided to stay and work on this one?"

"I'll stay." He looked at her and smiled. "There's something about the atmosphere that makes me want to stay."

"You wear a gun. Can you use it?"

"If need be. I'd prefer not to. But I've worn it since I was a youngster, riding range. I'd feel undressed without it."

"From what I hear, you made Sydney Berdue very uncomfortable without it. You're an unusual man, Mr. Canavan. Sometimes you sound like any cowhand,

and sometimes you come up with unexpected ideas and attitudes."

"Think nothing of it. When I was in Julesburg, the town drunk could quote Shakespeare by the hour. He'd been a professor at some eastern university until he got to hitting the bottle too hard. I punched cows on the range in Texas with the brother of an English lord."

"Are you suggesting you might be a duke in disguise?"

"Me? I'm just about what I seem. I'm a cowhand and a drifter. I spent a winter once snowed up in the mountains with two others just like me. We had four books, and by spring each of us knew them by heart, and we'd argued every point in them."

He changed the subject. "I hear there was a shooting in town?"

"Yes, and I am afraid it has started something nobody can stop."

"What sort of man was this Rolly Burt?"

"One of the best. You'd like him, and I did . . . I do. Hard as nails, loyal to a fault, but no youngster. He must be forty or better, but he says what he thinks and he thinks a good deal."

Canavan sipped his coffee and then said, casually, "Saw one of your hands in town the other day . . . At least he was riding a Box N horse, and I understand that's one of your brands. A tall, slope-shouldered man wearing a checked shirt. You know the one I mean?"

She looked straight at him, her eyes cool and direct. He had an uncomfortable feeling that she knew a lot more than he suspected. Of course, this was the man she had seen meet with Berdue at Thousand Springs. Probably she had overheard their conversation.

"Of course. That would be Kerb Dahl. He rides for us. Why are you interested?"

"Wondering about him. I'm trying to get folks placed around here."

"There are a lot of them trying to get you placed, too."

He laughed. "Are you one of them?"

"Yes, I believe I am. Remember, I overheard your conversation with your horse, and I am still wondering where you plan to be top-dog, as you phrased it."

"You shouldn't have heard it, and I am sorry you did. But I back down on none of it. I know how Reynolds got his ranch, and how Pogue got his. And neither has any moral or other claim beyond possession.

"You may have heard about what I told Reynolds in here the other night. I could tell him more, and I haven't started on Pogue yet. I'd just as soon you told no one that I intend to. He ran old man Carter off his place. Then he had Emmett Chubb kill Vin Carter. That's one of the things that brought me here."

"Revenge?"

"Well . . . I don't call it that. You might." He leaned toward her, eager for her to understand. "We don't have much law in this country. Local marshals take care of the crime in their towns, or they are supposed to. Emmett Chubb picked a fight with Vin when he was drunk . . . He didn't even know what he was doing. It was murder. But when the marshal came up, Vin had a gun in his hand.

"They called it self-defense, and Chubb actually laughed when they said it. No law could touch him, but there are other laws, the laws men make and adhere to in wild country. And one of them is the law of fair play.

"Sure, this is a rough country, and the men have rough ways. But most of them are basically honest. Nevertheless, we have a marshal here who was practically appointed by Charlie Reynolds. And the nearest court is approximately a hundred miles away and through Indian country.

"If we find a dog or a wolf with rabies, we kill him. If we find a man who kills wantonly, sooner or later he has to be killed. If two men get into a fight and all is equal, regardless of who is in the right, nothing is said—and this even though the skills of the two men may vary considerably. But if a man is shot in the back without a fair chance, usually action is taken on the spot.

"Vin Carter was my friend. He has no one else to act for him. He was not a gunfighter, only a brave young man who was a fair shot. But on the night he was killed, he was so drunk he could scarcely see. He had no idea what was happening to him, so it was murder.

"Perhaps before this is over, men like Chubb being what they are, I shall have the chance to even the measure with Chubb. I shall not have to seek him. Eventually, he will come to me. That is simply between us. The rest of it is something else.

"Pogue and Reynolds acquired their ranches through a ruthless use of power, of money and guns. And they are now in a feud. Neither of them has any claim on their property but possession. But when the shooting is over, there may be a different situation in the Soledad country. I shall have my ranch."

"Where, Bill?"

His pulse leaped at her use of his first name, the first time she had done so. He shrugged. "Let's wait and see."

The smile left his face. "By the way, as we parted the other evening a man made a point of saying you were a staked claim, and to stay away from you."

"What did you do?" Her eyes were thoughtful, curious, and somewhat amused.

"I told him he was a fool to believe any woman was a staked claim unless she wanted it so. He said, nevertheless, that you were staked out. If you are curious, you might as well know that I didn't believe him. Also," he smiled, "I wouldn't have paid any attention if I did."

"I'd have been surprised if you had." She arose, touching his hand lightly. "I must go now." He stood waiting as she said: "Nevertheless, Bill, what he said was true."

Bill Canavan's heart seemed to stop. "You mean. . . ? Well, what do you mean?"

"That I am engaged to marry Star Levitt. I have been engaged to him for three months." She turned quickly and was gone.

He stared after her. His thoughts refused to accept what she had said. Dixie Venable engaged to Star Levitt! So where did that leave him? Out in the cold, no doubt.

Well, he was used to that. It was often chilly where he was. Nevertheless, he was suddenly discouraged. When he had come to the Valley he had come seeking a ranch. What if he gained the ranch but never had this girl? A ranch by himself now seemed a very empty and lonely dream.

He dropped back into his chair. "Some hot coffee?" It was May, smiling down at him.

"Please," he said. And then he added, speaking softly into the empty air, "So that's the way it is? I find a girl worth having and she belongs to somebody else."

"Mind if I sit down?"

He looked up to see Allen Kinney, the hotel clerk, standing beside his table. "Please do," he said, "and have some coffee."

May delivered the coffee, and for a few minutes there was silence. "Canavan," Kinney asked suddenly, "you'd do a lot for a friend, wouldn't you?"

Surprised, he glanced up, and Kinney's eyes warned him of what was coming. "Why, sure!" And even as he spoke he was thinking over what was coming, for with a flash of intuition he guessed what Kinney had on his mind.

He should have known before this, for there was no other place. This was a Walt Pogue, Charlie Reynolds town.

"I've no right to ask this, but from the first you struck me as a man who went his own way, and who was not afraid. I consider myself a friend, whether you realize it or not, and somehow I feel we are on the same side. But I have no right to ask you to help, and you'd be sticking your neck out . . . way out."

"It's been out before. It's been out ever since I hit town."

"You have no local ties so far as I can see, and there's no one else I can turn to. And—"

"You're right. I have no local ties, and I just had the only possible one cut off short. What do you want me to do? Get him out of town?"

Kinney's cup almost dropped from his hand. "You mean—? You *know*?"

"I just guessed. Where else could he go? Is he hurt bad?"

"He can ride . . . I think. He's a good man, Bill, one of the very best. And if they find him they'll murder him. I had no idea what to do, and I know they will think of the hotel soon. It is a miracle that they haven't already."

"You've got him *here*?" Canavan was startled. "Then we'd best get him out tonight, while the getting is good."

"He's in the potato cellar, in a box covered with potatoes. It was all I could think of at the moment."

"Why me? How'd you happen to choose me?"

"Like I said, you've no local ties that I know of. And you have a way about you that speaks of independence. Then . . . May suggested it, and Dixie."

"She knows?"

"I thought of her first. The VV is out of this fight so far, and it seemed the only place. But she told me that although she would like to, there were reasons why it would be absolutely the worst place. Then she suggested you."

"*She* did?"

"Uh-huh. She said if you liked Burt you would do it. And you might even do it as a slap in the face for Pogue and Reynolds."

Canavan considered that. Without doubt Dixie had an idea of what was going on around the country, probably knowing a good deal more than anyone guessed. How many times might she have listened when the others plotted and planned?

"We can't wait. It will have to be done now. Have you got a spare horse?"

"Not that I can get without attracting attention. May has one at her place, out on the edge of town. The problem is to get him there."

"I'll handle it. You throw us together a sack of grub from the hotel restaurant's supplies. Do it without anybody knowing, if you can. When I come back to town, I can get what we need without questions."

Canavan got to his feet. "Get him ready to move. I'll get my horse down to May's and come back." He listened while Kinney gave him directions, then turned to the door.

It was too late.

A dozen hard-riding horsemen came charging up the street and swung down before the hotel. One man stepped up on the boardwalk and strode into the hotel. It was Walt Pogue. The man on his right was the man who had been with Berdue at Thousand Springs.

"Kinney! I want to search the hotel! That killer Rolly Burt is in town, an' by the lord Harry we'll hang him from a cottonwood limb before midnight!"

"Why would he be here?" Kinney spread his hands. He was pale, but completely self-possessed. He might have been addressing a class in history or reading a paper before a literary group. "I know Burt, but I haven't seen him. And why would he come here, of all places?"

Chapter VIII

Unobtrusively Bill Canavan was lounging against the door to the kitchen, his mind working swiftly. They would find Burt, and there was no earthly way to prevent it. There might be a chance to delay the hanging, if such it was to be. He had made up his mind there was to be no hanging. He knew nothing of Burt beyond the comments of those who mentioned him, but he sounded like the kind of a man Canavan liked. The very fact that those men were against him spoke in his favor.

"What you so worried about, Pogue?" he drawled.

Walt Pogue turned squarely around to face him. "Oh, it's you! What part do you have in this?"

"None at all. Just wondering what all the excitement's about. From all I hear, the man was attacked and he defended himself . . . did a mighty good job of it, too, I'd say. I'd say he did what a man should, and did it well. And he's no candidate for a lynching."

"He killed a Box N man."

"Seems to me a Box N man can die as well as any other. All three of them were grown-up men, and all three had guns—which makes it a fair fight. Seems kind of curious, too, why all the CR men are suddenly out of town. Are they that scared?"

"This is none of your deal!" It was the man from Thousand Springs. "Was I you, I'd stay out of what doesn't concern you."

Bill Canavan still leaned against the door, but slowly, carefully, contemptuously, he looked the man over, top to toe. Then he said gently, "Pogue, you've got a taste for knickknacks. If you want to take this boy home with you, you'd better keep him out of trouble."

Angered, the rider took a quick step forward. "All right, damn you! You're askin' for it!"

Pogue lifted a hand. "Forget it, Voyle! We've other fish to fry! You go look for Burt. I'll talk to Canavan."

Voyle hesitated, eager for a fight, but Canavan did not move, lounging carelessly against the doorpost, a queer half-smile on his face.

With an abrupt movement, Voyle turned away and spoke over his shoulder. "We'll talk about it another time, Canavan!"

"Sure," Canavan drawled lazily. And then as a parting he said softly, "Want to bring Dahl with you?"

Voyle caught himself in mid-stride, hunching his shoulders as if from an expected blow. He stopped then and stared back, shock, confusion, and uncertainty on his face.

Canavan looked over at Pogue. "You carry some odd characters. That Voyle now? Touchy, isn't he?"

Pogue was staring at him from under his brows. "What was that you said about Dahl? He's not one of my riders!"

"Is that right?" Canavan smiled, then shrugged. "Well, you got to admit I haven't been here very long, and I don't know who rides for whom around here. Somehow or other I figured Dahl an' Voyle trailed their ropes together."

Walt Pogue was annoyed and angry, and a little frightened. Why would Canavan tie those two together? Was he just talking or did he know something? How could he know anything? Another thought came to him. Where had Canavan come from, anyway? Who was he? What was he doing here, right now? So far as Pogue was aware, Dahl and Voyle were not even acquainted. Yet, thinking back to Voyle's startled reaction, he decided he did not like it, not any of it.

He walked to the coffee pot and filled a cup, adding cream and sugar liberally. Then he glanced over his shoulder at Canavan.

May had come up behind him. "He's gone!" she whispered. "He's not there!"

There was dust on her dress. He slapped at it, and she hurriedly brushed the dust away. "Where was he shot?" he whispered.

"In the upper leg, I think. He couldn't go far."

Pogue stared at them. "What are you two whispering about?" he demanded.

Canavan shrugged. "You *are* touchy. Can't a man talk to a pretty girl without you getting upset? I'd suggest you mind your own affairs."

Pogue put down the coffee cup. "Now you just see here! Nobody talks to—!"

"Pogue," Canavan said quietly, "if I were you I would think very carefully before you say anything more. I don't work for you, and it isn't likely that I ever will. And nobody tells me when to talk to a girl, or how I talk back to a man. So just back off . . . Back off, I say!"

For a moment, Pogue hesitated. He realized with startled awareness that he had brought himself to the verge of a gunfight with a man who didn't know enough to be afraid of him. For several years now he had talked just about as he willed, had run roughshod over many smaller men, and his manner had grown brusque and hard-shouldered as a result. A good man with a gun himself, he had come to rely on other men to do his fighting. Now, suddenly, he had talked himself into a corner, and he did not like having to back up. But wisdom advised it as the better way. After all, he now had too much to lose, while this casual drifter had nothing but his hide.

Pogue shrugged. "Damn it, man, with all this trouble around I'm getting jumpy. It's none of my affair what you two talk about."

Voyle came back into the room accompanied by two men. "No sign of him, boss, and we've been all over the place. We did find a box down under some spuds in the cellar. Might have been big enough to cover a man."

Allen Kinney had strolled back into the room, and Pogue turned on him. "What about that, Kinney?"

"Probably just something to keep the spuds off the ground," Canavan commented, to nobody in particular. "Damp ground will rot them mighty fast."

Pogue was angry. He started to say something, then thought better of it in time. Nor did Voyle have anything to say, and his eyes avoided Canavan's. The man was no coward, and it could only be that he was afraid of what Canavan might know. The allusion to Dahl had worried him. *He's mixed up in something he doesn't want his boss to know about,* Canavan told himself. *He's afraid I might spill the beans!*

Pogue turned and strode from the restaurant and out of the lobby door to the street, his men trailing after him. When the last man was gone, May turned to Kinney. "Allen, where can he be? He was there. You know he was there!"

"I know," Kinney agreed. "He must have heard

them and got out somehow. He'd be the last man to want to get any of us in trouble. But where could he go?"

Bill Canavan was thinking far ahead of them. The searchers would no doubt stop for a drink, but they would not stop long, and Pogue was there to make them get on the trail. Voyle apparently was not in on the plot to kill Burt, because he had been at Thousand Springs. Too little response had come from the CR, so it could have been a plot among Burt's own people to be rid of him. For some reason, Rolly Burt had become dangerous to them, and obviously it was intended that he die in the gunfight the previous night. Instead he had shot his way out of it, killing one of their men and wounding another. Now he would know that even his own outfit must be plotting against him, and he must be killed, and soon.

Yet Canavan was thinking beyond that. His mind was out there in the darkness with the wounded man. Enemies on every side, where could he turn? What could he do? How could he get away? What would he, Bill Canavan, do if he were a wounded man out there in the night with little ammunition and very little time?

He would have to hobble, or drag himself. He would be quickly noticed by anyone and investigated. He would not dare try to go far, and he must keep to the darkest ways, for there was enough light outside for a man to be seen.

Canavan, to whom every piece of ground was a potential battlefield, remembered the stone wall. It began not far from the hotel stables and fenced in a large orchard, planted long ago. Some of the stones had fallen, but it was still the best place around in which to fort up. Also it gave a man the shelter of darkness for about a hundred yards, no small aid to a man who must hitch himself along slowly.

Turning quickly, he went out the back door of

the hotel into the darkness. He stood for an instant to let his eyes grow accustomed to the night, and after a moment or two he could make out the stable and beyond it the wall.

Walking to the stable, he went along its side. Putting a hand on the stone wall, he vaulted easily over it. He stood still once more. If he approached Burt suddenly the wounded man might shoot, mistaking him for an enemy. And he did not know Burt, nor Burt him.

Moving stealthily, he worked his way along the wall. It was almost four feet high for most of its length, and there was a hedge of brambles and weeds growing close against it. He ripped a deep scratch into his hand, and swore softly, bitterly. Then he went on and was almost to the corner when a voice spoke from the shadows.

"All right, mister, you've made a good guess but a bad one. You let out one peep and the first one to die will be you!"

"Burt?"

"Naw!" The cowhand's tone was ripe with disgust. "This here is King Solomon, an' I'm huntin' the Queen of Sheba!"

"Listen, Burt, and get this straight the first time, because somebody else is going to do some guessing in the next few minutes. I'm your friend, although you don't know me. And I'm a friend of Kinney and May, from the hotel. I've come to help you get out of here. There's a horse at May's cabin, and we've got to get you there as fast as we can. And then get you out of town."

"How do I know who you are?"

"If I'd been with them I'd have yelled, wouldn't I?"

"You might yell once, but not more than once. Who are you? I can't see your face."

"You're aren't missing much. I'm Bill Canavan. I just blew in."

"You the gent who backed up Syd Berdue? Heard about that. A good job it was, too."

"Can you walk?"

"Give me a shoulder and I'll take a stab at it."

"Let's go then."

With an arm around Burt's waist, Canavan got him over the wall at its darkest place, then down a dark alley and over a fence. Then they faced open ground, but all in darkness, and beyond it a patch of woods and brush. Once under the shelter of the trees they would have cover all the way to May's house. If caught in the open there'd be nothing left but to shoot it out.

"All right, Burt. If a door opens anywhere, freeze."

"Where we goin'?"

"May's place, and her horse. Then we're taking to the hills. You know that old trail to the badlands?"

"Sure, but it's no good unless you circle around to Thousand Springs. There's no water. And that's a mighty rough ride."

"Don't worry about that. You get over there and lie down beside the trail. You hold up until you see me. I'll be riding an Appaloosa and leading her horse."

Burt's grip suddenly tightened. "Watch it! Door opening!"

They stood stock-still, no muscle moving, and then Burt's hand moved ever so carefully and it held a gun. He held it across in front of him, covering the man who stood in the light of the opened door. It was the bartender.

Somebody loomed over his shoulder. "Hey! Who's that out there?"

"Go back to your drinks," the bartender said. "I'll go see."

He came down the steps toward them, letting the door slam behind him. He walked straight toward them, and Canavan gripped his six-shooter.

As he drew near, Burt spoke. "Pat, you're a good

man, but you'd make a soft bunk for this chunk of lead."

"Don't fret yourself," Pat replied cooly. "If I hadn't come out, one of those Box N punchers would have, and there'd have been hell to pay. Go on . . . beat it. I'm not hunting trouble with either side." He turned his head to look at Canavan. "Nor with you, Bill. You don't recall me, but I remember you and that fuss you had with those Kingfisher outlaws. You boys get along now."

The fat man turned and walked back. They heard a drunken voice say, "Who was that? If it's that Rolly Burt, I'll surely—"

"Don't fret yourself," Pat repeated. "It's just a Mexican kid and a stray burro he's picked up." The door closed.

Canavan heaved a sigh. With no further talk they moved on, hobbling across the open stretch and into the trees. They heard a door slam, and angry voices. The town of Soledad would be an unpleasant place on this night.

When Canavan had the mare saddled, he told Burt: "If you hear anybody coming, get out of sight. When I come, I'll be riding that Appaloosa of mine. You'll know him."

"I've seen it. I just keep goin', is that right?"

"Right. And keep out of sight of anybody, and don't talk to anybody, and that goes for your CR hands as well. You hear me?"

"I surely do. They sure haven't been much help, at that. But I'll not forget what you've done, amigo, and you a stranger, too."

"Ride . . . Forget about me. I've got to get back into town and get my horse without exciting any comment. Once I get you where I'll be taking you, nobody will find you."

He watched the mare start off at a fast walk, and then he turned and walked back toward town. He heard shouts and yells up ahead, and then some drunken cowhand fired three times into the air. He saw the flashes.

Bill Canavan hitched his guns into place. He'd be lucky if he got out of town this night.

Very lucky . . .

Chapter IX

The disappearance of Rolly Burt was a
nine-day wonder in Soledad and the Valley country.
During the days following, Bill Canavan was in and
out of town several times, riding as he usually had but
avoiding all discussion of local politics and troubles,
of which he blandly insisted he knew nothing at all.

Burt had not been seen in Pie Town or anywhere
else around, nor were any horses missing. The search
pursued by the Box N hands had been intensive, but
turned up nothing at all. Rolly Burt, wounded, had
dropped off the end of the world.

Following the shooting and the search, Soledad
seemed abnormally quiet. Yet a rumor persisted that
with the end of the coming roundup, trouble would
come again and there would be nothing less than all-
out war between the two big ranches, with all out-
siders advised to keep out of the way and present a
low profile. For the time being, with the roundup in

the offing, both ranches seemed disposed to attend to first things first.

Second only to the disappearance of Rolly Burt was interest in Bill Canavan himself. He came and went around Soledad, but nobody seemed to have any idea who he was or what he was about. Yet whatever else he was doing, he was making friends among the small-fry and those businessmen who wished the troubles over.

Yet he remained a source of puzzlement to many, and especially to Walt Pogue, Charlie Reynolds and Star Levitt. And there was another who was even more curious and infinitely more wary. And that man was Emmett Chubb.

He first heard of Canavan's presence following the disappearance of Rolly Burt. The CR hands habitually ate at one long table presided over by Reynolds himself, and Syd Berdue invariably sat at his right hand.

"Hear Walt Pogue and his man Voyle had some words with Canavan," Reynolds commented to Berdue. "Looks like he's a man who makes enemies."

Berdue's comment was stifled by a sudden exclamation from down the table. Emmett Chubb put his cup down hard. "Did you say *Canavan?* Would that be Bill Canavan?"

"That's the man," Berdue looked down the table. "Do you know him?"

"I should smile, I know him. He's huntin' me."

"You?" Reynolds was relieved. "Why you?"

"Me an' a friend of his had a run-in. You probably knew him. Vin Carter."

"Ah? Carter was a friend of Canavan's?" Reynolds chewed in silence. "How good is this Canavan?" he asked suddenly.

Chubb waved a hand. "I wouldn't know. Down where he comes from, they set store by him."

A slim dark-faced young cowhand down the table drawled softly, "I know him, Emmett, an' if you tangle with him, be ready to go all the way. He's the gent who rode into King Fisher's hide-out in Mexico after a horse one of Fisher's boys stole off him. He rode the horse out of there, too, and the story is that he made Fisher take water. He killed the man who stole his horse. The fellow made a fool of himself and went for his gun."

"So he's chasing you, Emmett? That accounts for his coming here," Reynolds said. "I was wondering what he had on his mind."

"He might be here because of Vin Carter," Berdue suggested thoughtfully. "If he is, that could spell trouble for Walt Pogue."

In the days that followed Burt's escape from Soledad, Canavan was busy. He had roped and branded some of the wild cattle from the lava beds, and had pushed a few of them out on the range below Thousand Springs. There would be enough time later to brand more of them, but all he wanted now was for the brand to show up when the roundup started.

Astride the Appaloosa he headed for the VV. The morning was warm and pleasant, and he rode into the shade under the giant cottonwoods feeling very fit and very pleased with his world. Several of the hands were working around the place, and Kerb Dahl was there, mending a saddle girth.

Tom Venable was there, and his brow furrowed as he saw Canavan. He glanced quickly around, then walked to meet him. "Step down, won't you? Dixie has been telling me about you."

"Thanks. I will. Is Dixie around?" This was more than a chance to see Dixie, although that was always welcome. What he wanted more than anything was to simply look the place over and try to develop some idea of what was happening there.

"She's here," Venable said, then hesitated, making no move to tell him she had a visitor. "I say, Canavan, you're not coming with the idea of courting my sister, are you? You know she's spoken for."

"That's the impression everybody seems determined to sell me, Tom. I heard it first from Star Levitt."

"You mean he spoke to you about Dixie?"

"He did that. And then Dixie told me she was to marry him."

Tom Venable appeared to be relieved. That he had been worried was obvious. "Then you understand how things are. I wouldn't want any trouble over Dixie, and Star's very touchy."

Bill Canavan turned directly around to face Venable. "Understand this, Tom. Dixie has told me and Star Levitt told me, and now you have. Frankly, the fact that she is or seems to be engaged doesn't make a particle of difference. You don't need any long-winded explanations about how I feel or what my ideas are. When I am convinced she is in love with Levitt, I'll pull down my flag, but not until then. At the moment I don't believe she even likes the man."

Oddly enough, Venable did not become angry, nor did he attempt to argue the point. Yet the fact that he was worried was obvious. "I was afraid of that," he admitted. "I should have guessed." He was silent for a moment, and then said, "Be careful, Canavan. Be very careful, and I don't mean this as a warning to you. I don't want Dixie hurt. I don't want trouble."

"Now that you know where I stand," Canavan said bluntly, "are you going to get her for me, or must I go to the house for her?"

"To the house for whom?" They turned to see Dixie walking toward them, smiling. "Hello, Bill. Who were you coming after? Whoever could make your voice sound like that?"

"You," he said flatly, but smiling. "Nobody but you."

Her smile vanished but there was warmth in her eyes. "That's nice. You say that as if you mean it."

"I do."

"Boss?" A tall, lean, red-headed cowhand had come up to them. "Who has the Gallow's Frame brand?"

"Gallow's Frame? I never heard of it."

"Some big steers up near Thousand Springs. Wilder than all get-out. Some bulls, too, and a scattering of young stuff, all wearing a Gallow's Frame with a ready noose hangin' from it. We just barely got a look at the brand, but couldn't get anywhere near 'em."

"That's something new. Have you heard anything about them, Dixie?"

She shook her head, but there was an odd expression in her eyes. She glanced over at Canavan, whose expression was all innocence—combined with a slight twinkle that would have been a dead giveaway to anyone who knew him.

"No, I haven't seen them. Old steers, you say? Oh, by the way, Bill, you should meet Mabry, here. Bill Canavan is new to this country, Mabry, but I imagine he's interested in brands."

"Heard some talk about you," Mabry said, holding out his hand. "Seems you had a run-in with Syd Berdue."

Canavan noticed that Dahl's fingers had almost ceased to work on the girth, but his eyes did not lift, nor did he seem to be listening.

Mabry walked away with Tom Venable, and Dixie turned back to Canavan. "I thought you might be interested in meeting Mabry. He's a very good hand. He's also said to be a good friend to that cowhand they have been looking for in town . . . Rolly Burt."

Canavan offered no comment. There seemed to be nothing this girl did not know. She would be a good friend, but a dangerous enemy, for she was as intelligent as she was beautiful, and she seemed to miss nothing that went on. Was that just a casual comment about Burt? Or did she know something? Could Kinney have told her?

Of course, he recalled. Kinney had said she had suggested him, and now she was guessing. Nevertheless, it was good to know a man who was Burt's friend. He might need all the friends he could get before this was over.

Dahl's ears were obviously tuned to catch every word, so Canavan took her arm. "Shall we walk over and sit down?" He walked with her to a seat around one of the giant cottonwoods, but safely out of hearing.

"Dixie, I told your brother I did not intend to pay any attention to your engagement until I became sure you were in love with Levitt. Are you in love with him?"

She looked away from him, her face somewhat pale, lips pressed tight. She looked up at him. "Why else would a girl become engaged to a man?"

"I haven't an idea, yet there might be reasons." He glanced over at Dahl. "Until you tell me you love him, and look me in the eye when you say it, I'll play my hand the best way I can. I want you like I never wanted anything else in this world, and I mean to have you if you could find it in your heart to care for me. I'll not be asking you now. When I rode into this Valley I knew there would be trouble, and I thought I knew all the angles. I had studied the layout and I knew what I was getting into. Well, I discovered there's more going on here than I had any idea, and along with it, I found you. That I hadn't figured on, and it kind of throws a strange iron into the branding.

"Maybe you don't know all that's happening here. I suspect you don't, but I do think you know more than most anybody else. What I said when you heard me talkin' to Rio is true. I am here alone, riding for my own brand and for no other, and you've guessed right. For that Gallow's Frame brand is mine, and the noose is for anybody who wants to hang on it.

"Reynolds and Pogue are a couple of range pirates. They pushed out smaller, weaker men to get what they want, and now they're pushing at each other. Well, if they keep on they'll know they've been in a fight. I'm in this to stay, and I'm holding better cards than any of them know."

She had listened intently, her eyes looking off across the country. "You can't do anything alone, Bill! You must have help!" She put a hand on his arm. "Bill, is Rolly safe? I am not asking you where he is, just if he is safe. He did me a good turn once and he is an honest man."

"He's safe, and for your information, he's working for me now. He won't be doing much for another eight or ten days, and by that time it may all be over. How about this Mabry? Can he be relied on?"

"If he will work for you, he will die for you—and kill for you if it is the right kind of fight. He's Burt's best friend."

"Then if I can talk to him, you'll lose a good cowhand." He looked down at her. "Dixie, what's going on here? Who is Star Levitt? Who are Kerb Dahl and Voyle? I know there's a connection."

She got up quickly. "I cannot discuss that. Mr. Levitt is to be my husband."

His eyes went hard. "Not Levitt! Not for you! Anybody but him! And if you won't tell me, I'll find out anyhow."

He turned abruptly away and found himself facing, across the yard, Kerb Dahl and another man he had seen in town at the restaurant.

In that instant he became aware of many things. Tom Venable stood in the door, his face pale, eyes very bright. Kerb Dahl was on Canavan's right, holding his arms half-bent, hands swinging near his gun

butts. Behind him, Canavan could see the big old
tree with a rusty horseshoe nailed to its trunk. Two
saddled horses stood near the corral, and the sunlight
through the leaves dappled the earth with light and
shadow.

Behind him there was a low moan of fear from
Dixie, but Canavan did not move. He just waited,
watching the two men coming toward him. It could
be here. It could be now. This could be the moment.

Dahl spoke first, the shorter man moving a little
apart from him. Canavan remembered the girl behind
him and knew he dared not fight, yet some sixth
sense warned him there would be another man, a
third man hidden somewhere with a rifle. The difference.

"You're Bill Canavan," Dahl said. "You know me.
I'm Dahl. This is the first time you've come to the VV,
and we figure it will be the last. We don't want any
trouble-makers around."

Canavan weighed his words with care. If he said
the wrong thing, this could be a shooting match. He
did not like Dahl and was sure the other man was a
hired fighter, and ordinarily he would not have hesitated. Now, with Dixie somewhere behind him, he
dared not take the chance.

"Then keep your artillery handy," he said cooly,
"because I'll be back."

"You've been told," Dahl repeated.

Canavan studied them with cool contempt. He
knew they had expected a fight. They had expected
him to be as ready for battle as he'd been against
Berdue, and they planned to kill him. Yet he sensed
some relief in them, too, for despite the hidden rifle-
man these men were worried about their hides. He
was out of sight; they were on the firing line.

Mabry stood nearby as Canavan swung into the
saddle. Canavan spoke softly, so that only Mabry
could hear. "I've a job for you if you can get to town

in the next twelve hours. Meet me at the restaurant." He swung the Appaloosa around and added, "You might run into a friend of yours."

Mabry made no reply, and Canavan rode away knowing he was no closer to a solution of the situation at the VV than before. Mabry had simply stood there as if he, too, were warning Canavan away.

Canavan scowled in thought as he rode up the trail. There was an odd situation here, and he had believed he knew all that was going on in the Valley country. Actually, all he had known was the obvious, and there were many undercurrents here. On the one hand was Walt Pogue with Bob Streeter and Rep Hanson, two notorious paid gunmen. On the other side was Reynolds, with Emmett Chubb and Syd Berdue.

As for the VV, the Venables, who owned the ranch, seemed completely dominated by Star Levitt and their own cowhands. Levitt, it seemed, had a strong claim of some kind on Dixie herself, and what could be behind that? Whatever it was, it could make all the difference to him, not only for his plans for the Valley, but because of his love for Dixie.

Somewhere inside this patchwork of conflicting interests there lay another pattern, the pattern of that odd group he had seen meeting at Thousand Springs. At least one man from each ranch had been present. Dahl of the VV, Voyle of the Box N, Tolman of the Three Diamonds, and of course, Berdue from the CR.

Why that meeting? Voyle, from his actions, had not wished Pogue to know of it, and apparently Reynolds knew nothing. Who was behind it? What was behind it?

Whatever it was, it could make all the difference, for here was a situation within a situation, and just perhaps it was someone with the same idea he had, with a slight difference.

They might be thinking that when thieves fall out some other thieves might get their due.

They'd get something, Canavan promised himself. They would get what was coming to them . . . if he lived.

Chapter X

Quiet reigned at the Bit and Bridle when Bill Canavan rode into town in the late afternoon. He left his horse at the hitching rail and strolled through the half-open doors to the cool interior.

Only Pat the bartender was present. The room was dim and silent. Pat was idly polishing glasses when Canavan entered, but he glanced up and put a bottle and a glass in front of him. He had never cared much for whiskey, but it cut the dust from his throat and gave him a chance to stand quietly and think. Yet he had Pat to himself and this might be a chance to learn something.

"You've lived here a long time, Pat?"

"Uh-huh. I was here before Carter was killed. It was mighty good in the old days. No trouble. Once in a while some hand would come in and blow off a little steam, but nothing serious. I liked it that way."

"It's going to change some more, Pat. Quite a bit more."

"There's room for change, believe me. There's room."

"Where do you stand?"

Pat put the flat of both hands on the bar. "Not in the middle. Nor do I stand for Pogue or Reynolds or any of that lot. As for you, I am neither for you nor against you."

"You don't sound like much help."

"That's right. No help at all. I've got my saloon and I'm doing all right. I was here before either Pogue or Reynolds and I'll be here after they're gone."

"And after I'm gone?"

"Maybe that, too. You play your games with Pogue and Reynolds all you want, but you lay off Star Levitt and his crowd, d' you hear? They ain't human. They'll kill you like a cat would a mouse. They'll eat you alive."

"Maybe." Canavan sipped his drink. "Who are his crowd?"

Pat looked his disgust. "You've been to the VV. He runs that spread, so don't you be too friendly with that girl. She's poison."

Canavan offered no comment to that. Let Pat believe what he wished, he had his own ideas and his own judgment. It might be that feeling the way he did about her was the thing that would break him. He knew his own strength, and he matched with the strength of other men when the occasion demanded, but as yet there had been no real demand and he could afford to wait. When the showdown came he would push and push hard, and the showdown would come with the roundup if not sooner.

Pogue believed he had come to Soledad looking for Chubb. Reynolds and Berdue, despite their dislike for him, believed he was after Pogue, and each was prepared to keep hands off in the hopes that he would injure the other. Once they found his cattle on the range and realized he was making a bid for range, he would be in the middle of a fight with every man's hand against him.

Pat's warning was accurate, of course. Pogue and Reynolds were dangerous, but nothing to Levitt's crowd. Lifting his glass, Canavan studied his reflection in the mirror: the reflection of a tall, wide-shouldered young man with blunt, bronzed features and a smile that came easily to eyes that were half-cynical, half-amused.

A young man in a flat-crowned black hat, a gray shield-chested shirt and black knotted kerchief, black crossed belts that supported the worn holsters and walnut-stocked guns.

He was a fool, he decided, to think as he did about Dixie. What could he offer such a girl?

On the other hand, what could Star Levitt have to offer?

Nevertheless, he had come here to stay. When he rode the Appaloosa into the street of Soledad he had come to stay. He had known this was where it would all come to a head. Here he would establish himself or go down shooting. He considered his own plans and where he stood in his overall plan, and decided he had come further in less time than he had expected. In fact, he had one asset he had not expected to find.

He had Rolly Burt.

Camping on the mesa, the wounded man was rapidly recovering. With a single crutch he had whittled for himself, he could get around very well handling the camp chores, for he was not a man to sit idle, and he could fill Canavan in on the local customs and characters. Nights beside the campfire they had argued, yarned and just talked. Both had ridden for Charlie Goodnight, both knew John Chisum. They knew the same saloons in Tascosa, Fort Griffin and

El Paso. Both had been over the trail to Dodge and
to Cheyenne.

They talked the hours away of Uvalde and Laredo, of horses, cattle, camp cooks, of cattle rustling
and gunfighters until they knew each other and the
kind of men they were. Rolly Burt talked much of
Mabry. Mabry had told Burt that, much as he liked
both Tom and Dixie Venable, he must leave the VV
or be killed, for they tolerated only those hands
completely loyal to Star Levitt.

"Why were the Box N boys gunning for you,
Rolly?"

A frown gathered between his eyes. He shook
his head, obviously disturbed. "You know, I can't
figure it out. It was a cold deck, I saw that right at
the start. They had come to murder me."

"How'd you happen to be in town?"

"Berdue sent me in for a message."

"I see." He told Burt about the meeting below
Thousand Springs Mesa, and everything but Dixie's
part in it. "There's a tie-in somewhere. I think Berdue
sent you a-purpose, and he had those Box N boys
primed to kill you."

"But why? It doesn't make any kind of sense."

"Maybe it's something you know. Berdue is involved in some kind of a doublecross that he
doesn't want Reynolds to know anything about. He
probably is doublecrossing Reynolds himself, but it
looks like Star Levitt is the man behind the whole
operation."

"A deal between Levitt and Berdue? But they're
supposed to be enemies."

"What better cover could they have? You keep
an eye on the Springs, Rolly. They may meet again."

"Reminds me," Burt said, glancing up, "something
I've been meaning to ask. Several times I've heard a
funny kind of rumbling, sounds like it's coming from
the rock under me. Have you heard it?"

"I've heard it. Gives a man the creeps. Someday we'll do some prowling and find out what it is."

Standing now at the bar in the Bit and Bridle, Canavan went over the conversation. Yes, in having such an ally as Rolly Burt he was ahead of the game.

He turned his head to glance into the street. The day was gone, evening had come. He looked at the rose tint touching the clouds and felt a vague nostalgia for something, he knew not what.

Shadows were gathering between the buildings, but the faces of them, battered, wind-worn and dusty as they were, had acquired a kind of magic from the setting sun. At the rail Rio stamped an impatient hoof, and flipped his tail at a careless fly.

It was a quiet evening. How few of them there had been in those years behind him. And how many lonely nights . . . Restlessly, he turned back to his drink, scarcely touched. He wanted a home. It was all very well to ride the wild country. He had loved riding it and still did, but there was more to life than that. The empty people, they wanted nothing more; they chafed at bonds because they were not mature enough for discipline, the kind of discipline one gives himself. He had seen too many of them, sad, misguided people, railing at institutions and ideas they were too juvenile to accept. The important things in life called for maturity, for responsibility. Too many fled from it, wanting to be back in childhood when somebody else coped with the problems.

When he straightened up from leaning on the bar, his guns suddenly felt heavy on his hips. Someday . . . with any luck, things would be different.

Then the half-doors pushed open and Star Levitt came into the room. Tall and handsome, he stood against the fading light. For a moment he stood staring at Canavan, and then he came on into the room. He wore the same splendid white hat, a white buckskin vest, and gray trousers tucked into highly-polished boots. By comparison Canavan felt tired, dusty and wrinkled.

His manner was easy, completely confident. "Have a drink, Canavan?"

"Thanks, I've got one." In the mirror his battered shabbiness contrasted with the cool magnificence of Star Levitt. Gloomily, he stared at the reflection. What chance did he have, could he have, with a man who could look like that?

Levitt's smile was pleasant, his voice that of the conversation of every day. "Planning to leave soon?"

"I like it here," Canavan's own tone was dry. without interest or emotion.

"That's what the country needs, they say. Permanent settlers, somebody who will help to build the country. It is a fine idea, if you can make it stick."

"You're right, of course, but how about you, Levitt? Do you think you'll be able to stick it out when Pogue and Reynolds get to checking brands?"

The glass rattled in Pat's hand as he suddenly put it down on the back bar. Canavan felt a sudden harsh recklessness come up in his neck, a feeling such as he had never felt before. It was a mean, driving, ugly feeling, something this man aroused in him. But he had the play, and it was like him to push. "I've been out on the range of late and there's a lot of VV's made over into Three Diamonds, and Box N's to Triple Box A's, and they are both your brands."

It was fighting talk, and Canavan knew it. He had not wanted this, not right now, but there was an urge in him that drove him on.

Levitt was standing perfectly straight, looking at him through hard, level eyes. "That's dangerous talk, Cowhand! Dangerous for you or any other common drifter. You're getting into deep water, too deep for you to swim out."

"Let me be the judge. I've waded deeper water a few times, Levitt, and where I couldn't wade, I could swim. And if I couldn't swim I'd build some land under me."

Star Levitt's tone was calm, but the anger was plain and it was obvious he was a man not accustomed to being pushed or thwarted or even talked back to. He was a shrewd man, a planner, a conniver, but a man who liked to take his own time and do things in his own way.

In that moment Canavan learned something more about the man. For he had a temper, and when pushed he grew angry. Such a man might be pushed into hasty, uncalculated moves.

"All right." He was pushing again, pushing hard. "The other day you spoke about a staked claim. I am curious to see how well staked that claim is. I don't think you've staked it well at all, Levitt, and I want to see what will happen if somebody nudges those stakes a bit.

"You're a big man in a small puddle, Levitt, but you're not making the splash you think you are. Now you know where I stand, and we needn't talk in circles anymore. I am ready, Star. Are you?"

Before Star Levitt could reply, a new voice broke in. "Stand aside, Star, and let me have him!" Canavan felt the hair prickle along the back of his neck as he recognized Emmett Chubb. "I want him anyway, Star!"

Bill Canavan had not bargained for this. One of them, yes, but now he faced two of the deadliest gunmen in the west, and he was alone. Cold and still he waited, the air so tense he could hear the hoarse, frightened breathing of the bartender.

So still it was that all could hear Mabry's voice, low as it was. "If they want it, Canavan, I'll take Levitt for you. He's right under my gun."

Levitt's eyes did not waver. Canavan glimpsed the quick speculation in the man's eyes, the cool realization that the situation offered nothing for any of them. It was two and two, but Mabry's position outside the window clearly commanded the situation as he was behind both Levitt and Chubb.

It was Pat who broke the stalemate. "Nobody does any shootin' here unless it's me!" he said harshly. "Mabry, you stand where you are. Chubb, you take your hand away from that gun and walk right out the door, face-first. Levitt, you follow him. I ain't puttin' fresh sawdust on this floor again today. Not for nobody, I ain't!"

His command was reinforced by the twin barrels of a shotgun over the bar's edge, and nobody wanted to argue with a shotgun at that distance.

Chubb did not hesitate. He was too much the professional to like such a situation, so he turned on his heel and walked out without a word of protest.

Levitt held his ground a moment longer. "You talk a good fight, Canavan. We'll have to see what you're holding."

"I'll help you check brands at the roundup," Canavan said dryly.

Levitt walked out and Mabry put a foot over the sill and stepped inside. He was grinning. "Is that job still open?"

Canavan chuckled grimly. "Mabry, you've been workin' for me for the last three minutes!"

"You two finish your drinks and get out," Pat said. "Powder smoke gives me a headache!"

Chapter XI

They sat over their fire in the hollow on Thousand Springs Mesa, and the night was cool. The fire was small as they wanted no glow to attract attention to their hideout. Burt had elected himself camp cook, and he was making a stew. The coffee pot, blackened from many fires, stood in the coals on some flat rocks.

There was a smell of cedar smoke in the air and of crushed juniper. The night was still, with almost no touch of wind. The nearest ranch was at least ten miles away, and Soledad was much further. The sky was spangled with a million stars, and there were no clouds. Mabry leaned back on his saddle and clasped his hands behind his head.

"It surely isn't clear, what's goin' on," he said, "but it looks like Levitt is engineerin' some kind of a big steal . . . maybe cattle, maybe land, maybe all of it.

"From what you say, Voyle, Berdue and Dahl must all be in it with him, and I do know this. There's been a lot of hard cases comin' into the Valley lately, and not all of them are tied in with the CR or the Box N.

"Take Streeter an' Hanson now. They ride for Pogue, but are they really his boys? I think Streeter an' Hanson will stay out of it if Levitt says to. I think he's cut the ground from under both Pogue and Reynolds."

"The brands I saw aren't calculated to fool anybody, the way I see it," Canavan said. "I think they are planned to start trouble. It's my feeling Levitt wants to get them all together at the roundup and let the fight happen. Pogue and Reynolds are sore enough to be ready to bust loose and Levitt knows it. He and his boys can stand aside and just let them kill each other, then finish whoever is left."

"How many hands can Venable depend on?" Burt asked.

Mabry shrugged. "Three or four, but they are just good cowhands, not gunfighters. Dahl and his partner ran a couple of the others off, just made it so damn uncomfortable to work around them that they up an' quit. Now you lay the ground for it, I can see it was a planned thing."

"What goes on down there, Mabry? You've lived there."

"You couldn't prove nothing by me. Seems to be a lot of moving around at night, though. Several times riders have come in during the night and were gone before daybreak, leaving hard-ridden horses behind. Dahl and his partner always slept near the door, so it was them went to see what went on. I figured they were outlaw friends of theirs who needed spare horses." He looked over at Canavan. "After all, most of us know at least one gent who's on the dodge."

They talked quietly, letting tired muscles relax. Occasionally one or the other would move away from the fire and listen into the night. Despite the seeming security of their position, they were not trusting men.

Canavan took the plate he was offered and dished up some frijoles and beef, then added some of the stew. He could see but one answer. He would have to do some night riding. That also meant he would need more horses. In fact, they would all need them. He thought of the stock in the secret hollows in the lava beds . . . Some of them might have been saddle-trained. Yet, he might be able to get some stock from the Venables—very much on the quiet, of course.

"Roundup should start tomorrow," Burt commented. "Before it's gone very far we should know some of the answers."

From the rim of the mesa they watched the CR and Box N riders gathering cattle and starting them toward the roundup grounds.

The weather was hot and dry and dust rose in clouds. The cattle left the coolness and ample water of the Springs range with reluctance. As always it gave Canavan a thrill just to see the big herd bunched and moving. Even as a boy, when first he ran with the wild bunch, he had loved watching the big herds move, loved hearing the wild yells of the cowhands and the sudden dashes of the riders after bunch-quitters who wanted to head back to the rough country.

Regardless of their sympathies, there were good cattlemen on both sides and they worked hard, getting the wild stock out of the breaks and down on the flat to the sound of yells, good-natured argument and the usual joking. There would be several thousand head of cattle to be handled, and the roundup would move down-range before it was completed.

Yet as the day wore on there was a change. A sort of tenseness seemed to develop, and the riders tended to bunch with others working from the same ranch. It was coming, and the time had come to ride down there.

Mabry came up beside him. "Canavan? You want me to rep for you? Or will you tackle it yourself?"

Canavan considered for a moment. "We'll both go down, but we'll go loaded for bear."

"If a fight starts, what do we do?"

"Unless they start it with us, just pull out fast. We've no reason to fight at this point, but if we're down there somebody is liable to take a shot at us just for luck.

"Then when they find out that I've got cattle on this range, all hell is apt to break loose. So far they have me pegged as kind of an innocent bystander, but once they find I've moved in with cattle they will feel different."

"You may need help."

"Not yet. I don't want anybody killed. If the fight starts, just pull out fast."

It was daybreak on the second day that they rode down to join the working crew. Dixie was there, sitting her horse near Tom. "I may need some extra horses," Canavan said, "if I could borrow a few head . . .?"

"Sure," Tom said. "If you don't mind rough stock. Most of our lads have their own horses . . . I mean, the ones they prefer to ride. But I've got about sixty head corraled over in a box canyon back of our place. You can use any of them you like."

"I'll pick up about a dozen, if it's all right with you, and return them when the roundup is over."

Dixie glanced at him, but said nothing. He sat his horse, watching the work go forward. "Do you think there will be trouble?" she asked.

"Yes."

"You believe it was planned that way, don't you?"

"It was." He paused. "You may know more about it than I, and certainly you know more about the people involved. I don't want it to happen, although I've no regard for either Pogue or Reynolds. They've been riding for a fall, and this could be it."

"And what of you?"

"I want to be here . . . where you are."

She flushed. "Bill . . . please. You mustn't talk that way. There's too much . . . well, there are things happening that you don't understand. I don't want you killed."

"My kind don't kill very easy, Dixie, and I've got plans. I'll need more men, but I have two of the best."

Walt Pogue rode toward them. "Just seen Mabry. Is he workin' with you? I need a couple of good men and I'll pay top wages."

"No, thanks. I've come to rep for my brand."

Pogue's head bent forward like an old range bull about to charge. "Did you say . . . . *your* brand?"

"That's right," Canavan's face was innocent. "The Gallow's Frame."

The rancher reined his horse around so sharply that Canavan winced at the effect on the horse's mouth. "Who said you could run cattle on this range?"

Reynolds had come up in time to overhear. He looked as astonished and irritated as Pogue.

"It's government range," Canavan replied quietly, "and one man has as much right as the next."

"You'll find some difference of opinion on that!" Pogue said angrily. "This range is overcrowded as it is!"

"Tell that to Star Levitt."

They glared at him, yet neither spoke. The subject of Star Levitt was obviously not one they were prepared to cope with at the moment. It was Reynolds who finally replied. "He'll be dealt with. And from what I hear somebody is doing some fancy work with a runnin' iron."

Bill Canavan hooked his leg around the saddle horn. "Reynolds," he said gently, "you and Pogue better take a good, long look at those altered brands before you jump anybody. The first thing you will see is that whoever did it didn't give a damn whether you knew it or not. He's throwin' it right in your face, and just begging you to start something."

"I'll start something!" Reynolds flared. "Wait until this roundup is over."

"You throwin' that at me?" Pogue demanded. Fury was building up in the man, and as much of frustration as anger. Too much was happening, and he wanted to strike out in all directions, in any direction.

"You two ought to get down off your horses and fight it out," Canavan suggested. "Just get it out of your systems. Then maybe you can tackle your big problem. Or are you both afraid of Levitt? He's the one who's movin' in on you, and he doesn't even bother to bring his own cows, he just rebrands yours."

Canavan chuckled and Reynolds's face flamed. "We might get together, Walt an' me, just long enough to get shut of you!"

"Take first things first," Canavan said quietly. "You two are your own worst enemies, and next to yourselves is Star Levitt and his crowd.

"As for me, if you want some good advice, just leave me alone. I came here to stay. I've got cattle on this range and I intend to keep them there. I didn't ride in here by chance. I came because I knew you were going to kill each other off. I didn't bargain on Levitt doing it for me, but he will . . . if you boys don't beat him to it. But when you're all gone, I'll be here. If you want to fight, just start the ball rolling. But when you do, you'd better dig in for a long scrap because you'll get it, and I cut my teeth on range wars. If you want trouble, just cut loose your dogs!"

He dropped his leg, kicked his toe back into the stirrup, turned the Appaloosa and rode away.

Pogue glared at Mabry. "What's happening, Mabry? You've always been a good man."

"You listen to him, Walt. That's a mucho malo hombre, if you'll take it from me. He's got no reason to like either of you, but he's got other things on his mind now. If you want to know where I stand it's right beside him, me and Rolly Burt."

"Burt?" Pogue's face hardened. "Where is that murderin' son?"

Mabry looked around, his hand on the cantle of his saddle. "Pogue, why don't you find out why two of your men were gunnin' for him? I'll bet a paint pony you don't know! And Charlie, why don't you find out why none of your boys were in town to stand beside him? Why don't you ask your nephew why he sent him into town in the first place?"

"What's that? What're you gettin' at?" Reynolds demanded.

Mabry was riding away, and the older man stared after him. And for the first time he felt doubt as well as fear. What was happening? What did he mean by suggesting that he ask his nephew—

Mabry rode to where Canavan sat his horse. "Gave 'em something to worry over," he said cheerfully, and explained.

"That should do it. Their ears will be buzzing for a week . . . if they live that long." He gestured toward the cattle. "Some nice stock here, Mabry."

"How many head have you got out there?" Mabry asked.

"Not many. Couple of dozen, I'd guess. I wanted them to see the brand, that's all."

"What do we do now, Bill? Do we just wait?"

Canavan considered that. So far all had gone about as expected, yet he knew that a bullet . . . just one . . . could end it all. He was playing in a deadly game, but for high stakes.

"We'll sit tight now." He hesitated a moment and then said, "Mabry, I've got them cold-decked. I've got them whipped before they start, if I can just get out of this with a whole skin. I can't tell you what I've done, because I don't want to even think about it for fear they'll find out."

"What happens if they do? When they do?"

"There's only one thing they can do. They'll have to kill me. There won't be one of them against me, Mabry, it will be *every*one of them."

"Do you think Pogue and Reynolds can get through this roundup without a fight?"

"I doubt it. They're both too bullheaded, and there's hard feelings among their riders. Somebody will blow his top, and when he does there will be shooting."

Bill Canavan looked across the valley watching the familiar scene and feeling some of the old excitement within him. This was the roundup, usually the hardest work any cowhand had, although not necessarily the longest hours. His own longest hours had been on cattle drives, holding cattle after a stampede when he had already spent hours rounding them up. Usually the hands cussed the roundup, but they loved it, too. Hot and dusty, filled with danger from kicking hoofs and menacing horns or plunging horses, but filled with good fellowship, too, and comradely fun.

He watched the waving sea of horns where the gather was coming together. Every once in a while they would start to move out for somewhere, but a watching cowhand would turn them back again, and at such times there would be a ripple of movement along the sea of horns.

At the branding pens the sharp line of demarcation was broken by the business of the day, but otherwise the CR and the Box N held themselves apart. Because of this, or from wariness of what might happen, the VV riders did likewise.

Star Levitt, astride a magnificent white horse, was everywhere to be seen. For a time he was at the branding pens watching the action there, and then he was circling the holding herd where the cattle waited to be branded. Sighting Canavan and Mabry, he rode over to where they sat their horses, watching.

Canavan saw Mabry's face as Levitt started toward them. There was a cold, watchful quality about it, the sort of expression a man might have when he spotted a rattler approaching his bed at night.

"How are you, Canavan?" There was no indication in his manner that he had ever experienced the events that had taken place in the Bit and Bridle. He was cleanshaven as always, and as always he was immaculate. The dust of the roundup seemed not to have touched him.

Mabry, glancing at the two men, was struck by a striking similarity between them. Yet there was a subtle difference that drew him toward Canavan.

Both were big men, yet Levitt was both taller and heavier, and in the faces of both men there was strength and a certain assurance that set them apart. Canavan's manner carried a certain casual confidence that Levitt also had, but in a more brittle-seeming style than the rock-hard look that Canavan wore.

They were men shaped by nature to be enemies, two strong men with their faces turned in the same direction, yet guided by wholly different viewpoints and ruled by different standards. The one ruthless and relentless, prepared to take any advantage, and to stop at nothing. The other, hard, toughened by range wars and the brutally hard work of the western country, accustomed to the rough-handed fair play of the plains, yet equally relentless. It would be something to see, Mabry thought, if ever they came together in physical combat.

"Nice stock," Canavan commented casually. "You got many cows here?"

"Quite a few. I hear you're running the Gallow's Frame brand?"

"That's right."

"Strange that I hadn't heard of any cattle coming into the country lately. Did you pick yours up on the range?"

At many a time and in many a place, such a question could have led to shooting, but after his equally insulting comments in the saloon they were not important. These two knew their time was coming and neither was in a hurry. Levitt was completely, superbly confident, while Canavan had the assurance of a man who has faced many antagonists under many circumstances and always emerged a winner. Or usually. "No, I didn't need to. Your pattern suits you, mine suits me. My cattle were already here."

The remark drew the response he expected. "That's impossible! I know every brand that runs on this range, and there were only four until I moved in."

Canavan smiled enigmatically, knowing both the smile and the manner would irritate Levitt. "Star," he said, "you're a man who figures he's right smart, a whole lot smarter than other folks round and about. And you might be really smart if you didn't believe other people were so dumb.

"A man with your viewpoint doesn't have a chance to win, for that reason. You believe you're so much smarter than the opposition. You think everybody else but you is stupid as a month-old calf, so you ride into everything sure that everything will turn out right for you. You've the same fatal flaw in your character as most crooks, because they are incurable optimists.

"You came into this country playing it mighty big and strong. You were going to be the boss. You saw Pogue and Reynolds and you took them for easy marks. You seem to have had something on the Venables, but like so many crooks you overlooked the obvious.

"Let me tell you something, although you'll not believe it. You'd lost this fight before you ever took a hand in the game. If you were really as smart as you believe you are, you'd turn that horse of yours around and ride right out of here and never even look back."

Levitt smiled, but for the first time the smile was forced. Suddenly he was uneasy, yet it was only

Chapter XII

Canavan rode away, Mabry beside. Mabry stole a glance at Canavan. "You sure turned the knife in him. What you want him to do? Start something?"

"He's a planner and a plotter, Mabry. He works out a careful plan, but he's got too much temper for it. He'll get impatient, and maybe he'll do things he hadn't planned on. And if he does, he'll make mistakes."

He drew up and turned in the saddle to look back. Levitt was gone. "I wish I knew what he has on the Venables." He scowled. "You don't suppose she really likes him, do you?"

Mabry shrugged. "Sometimes I can guess what a steer will do, and I've even outguessed a wild bronc or two, but keep me away from women. I never could read the sign right, and every time I think I've got one figured, she crosses me up."

Despite the growing sense of trouble, the roundup was proceeding at a good pace. Yet it was like no roundup either Canavan or Mabry had experienced. The men were tense, less inclined to joke as the days went on, and conversation was at a minimum. Several times Canavan saw Dixie, but she avoided him. Tom Venable was there, sharing the work like any other cowhand, and proving himself to be not only ready and willing, but fairly knowing about cattle. It was obvious the hands liked him. He asked no favors but stepped up and did his share of the work and even a little more. From the first day, however, he had pitched right in and had worked hard, driving himself to keep up the pace set by the older, more knowledgeable hands.

He was a man to like, a man who could make a place for himself anywhere, so what was it with Levitt and him? Or her?

The days continued hot and dusty. Tempers grew short, but despite that fact there were no serious arguments or fights such as can occur on any roundup crew—and on some outfits are almost the order of the day. It seemed as if nobody wished to give offense, as if everybody knew something was about to happen and must be guarded against.

The next day, the roundup moved to the vicinity of Soledad, and there Canavan got his break. He had been trying to find a chance to talk to Dixie, and suddenly he saw it. She had been talking to Levitt, and she turned away from him and rode into the cottonwoods that bordered the VV ranch.

Canavan started after her and, looking around, saw himself watched by Dahl. His hard, lupine face—set in grim, watchful lines—was staring after him. Mabry was very much in the center of things, and working hard. Voyle had pulled out to saddle a fresh horse.

Dixie had gone but a few yards into the woods when he overtook her. For the first time, he noted how thin and pale of face she had become, and was shocked by the change.

"Dixie? Wait . . . I must talk to you."

She drew up and waited, although she kept her face averted and seemed in no mood for conversation. She made no comment as he came alongside, keeping her eyes straight ahead. "Leaving so soon?"

She nodded. "Star said the men were becoming quite rough in their language and would feel freer if I went in."

"I've been wanting to talk to you. You've been avoiding me."

She turned and looked straight at him then. "Yes, Bill, I have been. We must not see each other again. I am going to marry Star and seeing you simply won't do."

"You don't love him." The statement was flat and simple, but she avoided his gaze and offered no comment.

Then suddenly she said, "I've got to go, Bill. Star insisted I leave right away."

Canavan's eyes hardened. "Do you take orders from him? What is this, anyway? Are you a slave?"

Her face flushed and she was about to make an angry reply when the sense of her earlier remark hit him. He caught her wrist. "Dixie, did you say Star *insisted*? That you leave *now*?"

"Yes." She was astonished at his sudden vehemence. "He said—"

Her remark trailed off to nothing, for Bill Canavan had turned sharply in his saddle to look back toward the roundup grounds. Kerb Dahl had finished his cigarette. Voyle was fumbling with his saddle girth, and for the first time Canavan realized Voyle was carrying a rifle on his saddle within inches of his hands. Canavan's eyes searched for the white horse and found it beyond the herd.

He turned back to Dixie. "He's right. You ride for home and don't stop this side of there. No matter what happens, keep going!"

He wheeled his horse and cantered back toward the herd, taking a course that would keep him clear of Dahl and Voyle, hoping he would be in time. A small herd of cattle driven by Streeter and Hanson was drifting down toward the pens.

He drew up on the edge of the branding area just as Mabry straightened up to get the kinks out of his back. He had to call out three times before Mabry heard him and walked over. "Mabry, let's get out of here! It's coming! Now!"

Mabry wasted no time in talking. His horse was tied to the pens close at hand, and he was beside him in a half-dozen strides. He jerked the tie loose and swung into the saddle.

"Let's get out of here," Canavan said. "I don't know how or just where, but—"

At that moment, Emmett Chubb, sitting his horse, spoke irritably to Riggs, a young Box N rider. "You just naturally dumb or do ya have to try?"

Riggs looked around sharply. "What's that?" Riggs was puzzled. He was a tough youngster, hardworking and no nonsense about him, and Chubb's remark came as a complete surprise. Riggs was working hard while Chubb had merely lounged in his saddle, doing nothing. "What did you say?"

"Seems to me," Chubb drawled, "that you Box N boys done your best work before the roundup, slappin' brands on everything in sight!"

Hot and tired, Riggs was in no mood to be cautious or even to think. He had been insulted, and so had his outfit, something no self-respecting hand would allow.

"I said you were a bunch of cow thieves!" Chubb repeated.

"You're a liar!" Riggs shouted and, fast as Chubb was, he was only a hair faster than the angry young cowpuncher. Riggs's gun was coming up when Chubb's shot smashed him over the belt buckle. Riggs was knocked back two steps by the force of the bullet and his gun kept lifting, his blue eyes blazing with fury even as he died.

It was the signal for which they had waited, and in an instant the branding pens were thundering with gunfire. Hot stabs of flame penetrated the dust. Men screamed, cried out and went down, groveling in the dust, struggling in their last bitter gasp to get off a shot, at least one shot.

Mabry came around the corner of the pens on a dead run. Canavan gestured toward the timber. "It's their fight!" he yelled. "Let them have it!"

"Look!" Mabry was pointing.

Streeter and Hanson, on the ground behind their horses, were shooting across the saddles, opening up on Pogue and Reynolds. Voyle was dodging through scattering cattle, six-gun in hand, trying for a shot at someone. From the dust came a scream of agony, then a bullet cut the scream off short.

"Pogue's own men turned on him!" Mabry yelled angrily. "Did you see that?"

"We'd better light a shuck. I think they intended to nail us, too!"

They had been off at a dead run, and now their horses broke into the trees and they pulled up to look back. The crash and thunder of the guns had ceased. A riderless horse ran from the dust, stirrups flopping against its sides. Somewhere in the dust there was a single shot . . . then another.

Only when they had put miles behind them did they slow up to talk. Mabry glanced at Canavan. "I feel like a coyote, runnin' off from a fight like that, but it surely wasn't our fight."

"It wasn't supposed to be a fight. It was a massacre, and Levitt engineered the whole affair." Canavan explained how Dixie had been started home to get her out of harm's way before the shooting started. "Chubb had his orders, and he deliberately started that fight when he got the go-ahead signal."

"Riggs was a good hand. One of the best men on a horse I ever did see."

"There was nothing we could have done but stay there and die. He had all his men in picked firing positions and they had no idea of letting anyone get away."

"Do you suppose anyone did?"

"Doubt it. Not unless he was shot with luck. I think those last shots we heard were Levitt's men going around killing those who were still alive."

Canavan stopped his horse and turned to look back, to study his back trail with care. By now Levitt would know they had escaped the massacre, and he would have men hunting them, for none must be left to tell the story.

"Mabry, from now on you and me will have to ride carefully every step of the way. We saw what happened, and if ever the law comes in here they'll be asking questions we can answer. So Levitt will want us dead.

"But somehow we've got to survive. We've got to get the Venables out from under him, and we've got to see that Levitt gets what he deserves."

"Reynolds and Pogue only got what they had comin'," Mabry said. "I feel no sorrow for them. What I'm wonderin' is what Levitt will do now? He's got the Venables under his thumb and the range sewed up."

Canavan considered that and thought he might have the answer. "We'll have to wait and see. He'll blame the fight on the feud between the two big outfits and claim he was only an innocent bystander."

"What about the riders? Some of them will tell the truth."

"If they know it. We knew what was coming in time to pull out, but down there among the dust and the confusion they'd have no chance to even see who started it. They were busy working, and all of a sudden the shooting began, that's all they'll know. And if anybody is damn fool enough to start asking questions, he won't last long."

"If he kills like that," Mabry wondered, "what chance have we got?"

"A good chance if we can keep out of sight. We're honest men, even if the only law here is gunlaw. We'll have to wait and see what the next move is, but I'm guessing Levitt will clean up all the loose ends. And then he might even call in the law from outside to give himself a clean bill."

Rolly Burt was waiting for them when they reached the mesa. He glanced from one to the other. "What happened? You boys look like you been runnin'."

As briefly as possible, Canavan explained. "The fight might have come, anyway, even if Levitt hadn't planned it, but without planning he couldn't be sure the right men would be killed."

"How many were down?"

"No tellin'," Mabry said. "Enough to leave Levitt in the saddle, playing the big, honest man who only wants to keep the peace. There was too much confusion for good shooting, except by those on the fringe where his men were."

Burt began dishing up the food. "Bill, what happened to Charlie Reynolds?"

"He's sure to be dead. He and Pogue. Even Berdue was shooting at them, at his own uncle. No man deserves that."

When they were sitting around the small fire eating, Burt said, "Got some news of my own. Whilst you two were gone, I did some stumping around here, trying to loosen up the muscles in my game leg. You'll never guess what I found."

"What?" Struck by something in Burt's tone, Canavan paused with a forkful of beans almost to his mouth. "What did you find?"

"That rumblin' in the rock? I found what causes it, and man, when you see it your hair'll stand right on end. You never seen anything like it!"

Chapter XIII

Bill Canavan opened his eyes to look up through the rustling aspen leaves at a vast expanse of impossibly blue sky spangled with white puff-balls of cloud. He rolled out of his blankets and started to dress, trying to keep his feet out of the grass, still wet with morning dew.

Mabry stuck his head—bristling with a wild mat of red hair—from under his blanket and stared unhappily at Canavan.

"Rolly," he complained, "what can a man do when his boss insists on gettin' up so early? It ain't neither fittin' nor right for a man to get up at this heathen hour, not when there's no stock to feed."

"Pull in your neck then, sorrel-head!" Canavan growled. "I'm going to take a look at the valley, and then Rolly can scare up some chuck."

"How about that rumblin'? I heard it again last night. Gives a man the creeps."

Burt sat up and rubbed his unshaved jowls, looking around for his boots. "Damn it," he muttered, "I need a shave."

"Never seen you when you didn't." Mabry thrust his thumb through a hole in his sock and swore, then pulled it on. "You need a haircut, too, you durned Siwash! Ugly, that's what you are! What a thing to see when a man first wakes up! Lucky you ain't never hitched with no gal. She'd surely have nightmares, just lookin' at you!"

Canavan left them arguing and, taking a cup of coffee, went to the nest of boulders he used for a lookout. Taking a careful look around, wary of any visiting rattler or scorpion, he sat down and, putting his cup on a flat rock, took his field glass and began a study of the country below.

At first all seemed serene and lovely. Morning sunlight sparkled on the waters of the pool below, and he could hear the pleasant sound of running water. The air was exceptionally clear, and there was no sound. Then some distance off, he heard a cow bawl.

The sun felt good on his back, and he shifted a little and pointed his glass once more. Instantly, he froze. A group of riders were coming up the trail toward Thousand Springs, riding slowly, as if tired. Star Levitt was not among them . . . at least, there was no white horse and no white hat.

As they drew nearer he made out Syd Berdue, Emmett Chubb, Kerb Dahl and Voyle. He did not know the others, although he had seen them around. They drew up right below to let their horses drink. And on this morning, they were not speaking in the low, conspiratorial tones as before, and he could hear them plainly enough.

"Beats all, what happened to him!" Voyle complained irritably. "One minute they were both there and then they were gone."

"We'd better find 'em," Dahl replied. "I never did see Star so wrought up about anything as when he found they'd gotten away. He must have turned over everything on the flat, hunting them. He just refused to believe they'd not been killed. Man, I never seen anybody so mad!"

"He's a bad man to cross," Streeter added. "When he's mad he goes crazy."

Chubb hung back from the group, taking no part in the conversation. From time to time his eyes went to Berdue. From where he lay among the rocks, Canavan could not see his eyes, but he could see the turning of his head. Getting down, Chubb walked to the springs for a drink, and when he stood up he wiped his mouth with the back of his hand.

He took out the makings and began to build a smoke. "Some things about this here that I don't like," he commented, after a bit.

There was no reply, but Canavan had an idea he was expressing a feeling that was pretty general. Syd Berdue idly flicked his quirt at a mesquite.

Berdue looked up. "At least you can't say he isn't thorough!" he said dryly.

Chubb looked around, then spat. "He's thorough, all right! Almost too thorough! He had me primed to start the action by picking a fight with Riggs. He had Riggs pegged as a hothead who would blow his top first thing. Well, I had no use for Riggs. He rubbed me the wrong way, and we'd likely have been in a fight sooner or later anyway. He never said a word about what was to come after, and it was pure luck I didn't get killed!"

Streeter nodded. "I had three targets laid out for me. I was to kill Reynolds and then get some lead into Pogue if time allowed, and even if somebody had beat me to it."

Hanson chuckled without humor. "I was to kill Pogue, then take a shot at Reynolds. Then I was supposed to turn my gun on Jason Farmer. Farmer was a tough man who'd been with Pogue a long time."

Dahl changed the subject. "Where d'you figure Canavan went?"

"Where did Rolly Burt go?" Voyle asked. "If you ask me, that Canavan's no fool. Mabry and him got shut of those brandin' pens in a mighty big hurry! I never figured either one of them would run from a fight."

"You got to ask yourselves whose fight it was," Streeter commented. "It surely wasn't theirs. Canavan made it plain he had no use for either Pogue or Reynolds, so he'd be a fool to get shot up for either of them."

"Might have left the country," Voyle suggested.

"I doubt it," Chubb said quietly. "Canavan's after my scalp. I killed a friend of his. He wouldn't leave without tackling me."

"Pity he couldn't have done it earlier," Voyle said. "It would have saved us a lot of riding."

"He's tough," Streeter said. "He jumped the boss a couple of times. Pogue, too. He don't seem to take water for anybody."

Syd Berdue turned to look at them, waiting for somebody to mention his own meeting with Canavan, but they avoided it.

"I'd say the thing to do is stop chasing around the country looking for him and just keep an eye on that Kinney feller at the hotel. Seems to me they were all-fired friendly."

"Wonder where Canavan come from?" Voyle asked.

"Used to be down in the border country," Streeter said. "Had quite a name down there."

"Gunfighter?"

"Well . . . not really. But as a fighter, yes. He had the name of a man to leave alone. He was a bronc fighter, wild-horse hunter. But he'd ridden shotgun on stages and such-like."

"He was friendly with that Venable girl, too,"

Voyle said. "I think the boss is buckin' a stacked deck there. I don't think she's got any use for him."

Canavan's eyes were on Dahl, who hovered in the background listening but offering no comment. Very likely he would go to Levitt as soon as they rode in and repeat every word. Dahl had not been planted on the VV for nothing. All of them were talking too much, and Levitt was not a man who would like loose tongues.

How many of them would be allowed to remain alive once Levitt had accomplished what he wanted to do was something else. From his viewpoint there would be no sense in having men around who knew too much, for the country was changing and new people would soon be moving in, crowding out the wild elements, bringing with them churches, schools, banks and more ordered ways of business.

This Star Levitt knew, and he hoped to have himself firmly established before such a change took place, the owner of vast lands with no one to question his right or how the lands had been acquired.

There was more talk and he listened, but heard nothing of importance. He watched until they rode away, following some lead they believed they had. In the future, Canavan decided, he must be more careful. There must be no trail to be followed, and the path up the mesa must be blocked off or watched.

Long after they rode away he lay waiting, hoping for some sight of Dixie, but there was none. Either she was too closely watched or she had not suspected this meeting. More than he liked to admit, he was worried. Star Levitt had revealed himself as a more ruthless man than anyone had suspected.

Of them all, perhaps Emmett Chubb's judgment of the man was the most accurate. There was small chance that anyone would escape the Valley to repeat what they knew when, sometime, they had imbibed too freely. No doubt he had not been merely careless in not warning Chubb of what was to happen, for

Levitt knew full well that the massacre at the branding pens would eliminate his most formidable rivals.
And if Chubb or a few others were killed in the cross-
fire . . . who was to care?

There was little Canavan could now do until
Levitt's next move was revealed. All they could do was
sit tight and try not to be found. As long as they were
free, Star Levitt's plan was incomplete, and they
would be a constant worry. Yet Reynolds and Pogue
were gone and the Valley ranches lay right in Levitt's
palm, or so he would believe. Of course, he actually had nothing, for Canavan held the water rights.
Levitt, with his penchant toward the illegal and the
use of the strong hand, had undoubtedly not even considered such a possibility. Most land in the west was
held by squatter's right, and the idea of acquiring land
by legal means almost unknown. The land was there
for the taking, and most men looked upon it as they
did the buffalo or the trees they so freely cut down
as theirs by right of discovery and use.

Returning to the fire, he ate a late breakfast and
sat talking over coffee. Finally, he said to Burt, "All
right, we'll see what you've got to show us, then Mabry
and me will go down into the lava beds and push out
some more cattle. Nothing like giving Levitt something
to worry about."

"You be careful," Rolly warned. "He's smart as an
old fox. All the time you're making your plans, he's
probably thinking away ahead of you."

Rolly Burt, whose leg was almost back to normal,
led them through the aspens to the open mesa, and
then along its top toward the jumble of boulders that
blocked off any approach from the northwest except
by the narrow trail they used in coming and going.

The way Burt took was a dim path, long unused,
that led them into a maze of boulders and great,
broken slabs of rock. Several times, Canavan stopped
to look around. He knew little of such things but it
appeared to be an old earthquake fault, where in

some vanished time the rock itself had fractured and split. The vague path ended at a great, leaning slab of granite under which there was a dark, ominous opening. They hesitated, not liking the looks of the place, but Rolly went on.

"Come on! You ain't seen nothing yet!" He had brought with him several candles, and he passed one to each of them. "Found these in the stores you hid up here," he commented, "and we'll never need them more than here."

He stooped and went into the opening. A moment longer Canavan hesitated. He had no liking for holes or cramped places, but he ducked his head and went in, almost at once feeling a sense of space around him, and he held his candle high as Burt was doing and looked down a steep floor that fell away before them in a long, gradual descent. Far away in the abysmal darkness they heard faintly the sound of falling water.

The air was damp and cool, a faint breeze coming from somewhere deep within the mountain. Yet this was no narrow passage in which he found himself but a vast cavern where Burt led them, hobbling with his single crutch, deeper and deeper into the mountain.

They had descended seventy or eighty feet below the level of the mesa's top when he paused on the rim of a black hole. Leaning forward, holding his candle out, Bill Canavan found himself looking into a vast, bottomless depth from which there came at intervals a weird sighing and a low rumble.

"We've got maybe ten minutes, the way I figure it. Then, to be on the safe side, we've got to get out." He knelt and touched the rock at the edge of the hole. "Look how smooth! Water done that, water falling on it, water running over it for maybe thousands of years.

"I tried to time it yesterday, an' it seems to come about ever' three hours. Pressure must build away down inside the mountain and then she blows a cork an' water comes a-spoutin' out of this hole. She shoots clear up nigh to the roof, an' she keeps spoutin' for three, four minutes, then it dies away and that's the end."

"I'll be doggoned!" Mabry exclaimed. "I've heard of this place! Injuns used to call it the Talking Mountain! Folks were warned to stay clear away from it. Said it was a death-trap!"

"When she shoots up," Burt said, "stones come boilin' up with it, too, an' water fills this room and turns it into a huge whirlpool. But that ain't all. Look up yonder!" He stepped back and pointed up.

High above them in the vaulted top of the cave, they could make out several ragged holes where a vague light filtered in. "They seem to be well back in the trees, but a man could walk right into one of them if he wasn't careful. If the fall didn't kill him he'd be trapped here when the water came."

They turned and started back, yet they had taken no more than a step or two when from beneath them they heard a dull rumble.

"*Run!*" Burt's face was panic-stricken. "Here she comes!"

He broke into a limping run, then tripped and fell full length on the steep upward trail. Canavan stooped and lifted him, but Rolly Burt was a heavy man and had not Mabry grabbed the other arm he would never have gotten him up the steep trail in time.

Plunging ahead, they scrambled to the top and out of the cave only just in time, bursting into the sunlight, faces strained and pale. Behind them they heard the roar of water and the pound and rumble of boulders battering the cave walls and even the roof.

For several moments they stood panting and listening to the rumble from down below. Slowly it died away, and then there was no sound.

"That," said Mabry, "is a good place to keep out of!"

When they returned to the camp, Burt started for his horse. "I'll saddle up and help you gents. I've been loafin' too long!"

"You stay here and keep an eye on the Springs. I've a hunch we're going to have more visitors and I want to know who they are. Anyway, this is a two-man job. If we need help tomorrow, we'll leave Mabry behind and you can have a go at it."

Mabry had little to say on the ride to the lava beds, and Canavan was just as pleased, for he had much thinking to do. Dixie's situation worried him. No doubt foolishly, for if she was to marry Star Levitt she was probably safe enough. Nonetheless, with such a man one never knew, and by this time she had undoubtedly realized the reason for his hurrying her away from the roundup. Canavan made up his mind that if it could be done, he would slip into town and have a talk with Kinney, or with May.

If he could reach neither of them, he might make a contact with Scott, whom he had scarcely seen since arriving in Soledad. After all, no progress reports were needed because Scott would know, as did everyone else, what was happening in the town and in the Valley. After all, Scott was the better choice, for judging by what he heard at the Springs, Kinney might be watched and Canavan had no desire to get the man in trouble.

He was eager to know what was happening in Soledad and on the VV, and to be cut off from news was maddening. He found himself thinking of Dixie in almost every waking moment, and it was frustrating to realize that he could not see her or hear of her.

The work in the lava beds was hot and rough. The wild cattle were big and they were mean. They had run wild too long, and they wanted no part of a rope nor of a man. Throwing and branding them was slow work for two men, and was hard on their horses. They did succeed in trapping a dozen wild horses, two of which carried brands and old saddle marks and had evidently been ridden. Both reacted well to the rope, ceasing to fight as soon as it settled on their shoulders.

Mabry saddled one of them and he bucked a little, then settled down, and he topped off the other one who wore a brand. Both were good stock, and one of them gave some evidence of being a cutting horse, which they could well use.

For several days they worked the cattle in the lava beds, and took time out to rough-break two more of the horses. "We'll take 'em out tomorrow," Canavan suggested. "You keep watch and I'll ride out and scout around to see if we've had any visitors while we've been in here."

"Burt will be worried," Mabry thought.

"Don't worry about him. He'll have figured out what we're up to."

Nevertheless, Canavan knew that Burt would be worried. They had not expected to be gone so long, and when a man is alone his imagination can build up all sorts of troubles and worries—just as his own was now doing with the situation in Soledad.

Leaving Mabry with the rounded-up cattle in their improvised corral, he went up the notch and worked his way back through the maze to the outer Valley. Once there he drew up and listened for a long time, yet he heard no sounds not normal to the night, and he rode on, glancing from time to time at the mesa's rim. What he expected to see he did not know, but hoped he would see nothing.

If he intended to get any sleep he must start back, but there appeared to be nobody around, and they could probably drift the cattle into the valley and scatter them out without being observed. After that they would return to the mesa and Rolly Burt.

His eyes strayed off toward Soledad and the VV. Was she all right? Was she thinking of him? Did she ever think of him? Gloomily, he reflected that he had built a lot of hopes on very little. After all, she had said nothing that even suggested she cared for him. That she called him by his first name meant nothing in western country, where first names were habitually used. They had talked, and they seemed to have things in common but who was he, after all? No more than a drifting cowhand looking for a place to light, and willing to use a gun to find it. Not a reassuring pattern for a man with whom to live out the years.

Star Levitt was a big, handsome, well-dressed man with a certain amount of polish and an easy way with people. He had the advantage of being where he could see Dixie every day, where they could talk and become acquainted. After all, how did he, Bill Canavan, know what type of man Dixie would prefer? Were not all his dreams built on a lot of wishing and dreaming?

"Rio," he said at last, "maybe this isn't where we light, after all. Maybe this is just one more stop on a long, long trail." The horse twitched his ears, stomped a foot and blew through his nose, all of which might mean anything or nothing.

The trouble was that he did not want any more long, long trails. Not at least without having somewhere to come back to, or someone. There had been too many of those long, lonely trails, too many empty nights, too many places where he did not belong, where he had no one or nothing.

He rode back through the notch to the camp. Mabry was already asleep, although he opened his eyes, grunted a little and returned to sleep.

Canavan added a few sticks to the fire and tasted the coffee. Lukewarm. He put the pot back on the coals and pushed more coals around it, adding a little water, but not too much.

He went out and stripped the gear from the Appaloosa and turned the horse loose to graze. The moon was rising and the weird rocks along the rim raised their gargoyle-like heads, seeming to peer over the edge into their lost and lonely valley. He was uneasy.

Nothing could find them here, but nonetheless he was restless and felt little like sleeping. He dug out a couple of dry biscuits and ate them while he drank his coffee.

His thoughts returned to Star Levitt. Who was the man? Where had he come from and what ill wind brought him to this place at this time? He seemed to be an easterner, but he knew too much about cattle and ranching for that. The guns he wore had seen use, and they alone struck an incongruous note, for they were much worn from constant wear and much use.

The west was not so large a place as many seemed to believe. The country was enormous, but the population was not, and the men who rode the wild country knew each other, at least by hearsay. Among the gun-packing fraternity—those who lived by the gun either on the side of the law or against it—all knew each other by name and reputation. At every camp fire there was discussion of their respective abilities.

So who was Star Levitt? Where had he come from? And what name had he sometime used? Or was he from elsewhere? The east had its gunfighters, too, although most were duelists or riverboat gamblers. There was McClung, for example, who was reputed to have killed more than a hundred men . . . And there were others.

Clay Allison was ranching in New Mexico now, and Hardin had gone to San Antone—or was said to be there, the last Canavan had heard. John Slaughter was too short to be Levitt, and he was an honest man, anyway. One by one he turned them over and over in his mind, but came up with no answers.

At daybreak, after a restless night, he was in the saddle once more, and with Mabry he pushed the unwilling steers through the notch and out into the wider world of the Valley. Moving along, they scattered the cattle so as not to make it too obvious where they might have come from, and they dusted over their trail out of the lava beds.

Rolly Burt had a fire going when they rode in, hot and tired after the drive. Hot food was ready and fresh coffee, and he let them eat before he talked.

"Took a chance last night," he said, "and rode into Soledad."

They both looked up sharply. "You *what?*" Mabry said.

"Rode in," he repeated smugly. "Goin' stale lyin' around with time on my hands, and I figured to find out what the situation was. There've been some changes made."

"What's happened?" Canavan's irritation at Burt's ride was lost in his desire for news.

"Levitt's been havin' everything his own way, of course, and he's been makin' it pay. He got two or three folks together and they made Emmett Chubb marshal, and the word is that he's going to be almighty strict and stern until they get rid of the lawless element that's been making the trouble. From the way they talk, that seems to be us.

"I talked to Scott and he sure enough wants to see you. Dixie Venable ain't been seen in town since the big fight. And Tom's been in only once, and then he high-tailed it back to the VV almost right off.

"Levitt has sent for outside law. He says he wants this Pogue-Reynolds feud cleared up and the blame put where it should be, right on your shoulders."

"*Mine?*"

"Well, he admits there was a feud before you came, but he implies you stirred it up. He also says there's been some rustling going on and he lays that to you. Also," and here Burt cleared his throat, avoiding Canavan's eyes, "the word is out that there will be a weddin' out at the VV right soon."

Bill Canavan stared into the coals. So there it was. The end to dreams. Now Levitt would marry Dixie

Venable and the VV would be his in all but name . . . perhaps even that, too.

Yet what could he do? What could anybody do? That Levitt would succeed in making him an outlaw was one thing he had not expected. And if anything was to be done to change that, it had better be done soon.

"There's some other talk around. Seems Syd Berdue is kind of unhappy the way things turned out. Chubb is marshal in town, an' Kerb Dahl is foreman at the VV. Bob Streeter is foreman over at the CR, but Levitt has told Berdue he'll be taken care of."

"That's maybe what's botherin' him," Burt said dryly. "I know how I'd feel if Star Levitt said I was to be taken care of. I'd either take a shot at Star, or a fast horse out of the country."

"Well, Berdue ain't leavin'. Not so's you'd notice it. I reckon Star is anxious to have everything lookin' all clean and pretty for this law he's invitin' in. The Deputy U.S. Marshal who will come in—or deputy sheriff, whichever it is—he ain't going to look very far if things seem to be all cleaned up and under control."

Canavan pondered the situation. Certainly, Levitt's position was good. He was a smooth, easy-talking man of impeccable appearance, and if everything was outwardly calm and he had a plausible story to tell, any outside investigation was likely to be shelved.

The Valley would then be safely in Levitt's hands, and no doubt he would have declared Bill Canavan an outlaw, and his friends likewise. He could then be hunted down and killed with no questions asked.

His own position was legally strong. If he could only meet with the officers when they came in . . . Levitt still did not know that he held the water rights for the entire Valley, and if Canavan could only reach the officers, he could present his own case and demonstrate that Levitt was at best an interloper.

Now was the time to come down off the mesa. He

had to move into the arena before Levitt could consolidate his position. The idea came to him suddenly, and he knew exactly what he would do!

"There's talk around about those steers of yours," Burt added. "There's a lot of argument where they came from. They are full-grown steers wearing no other brands but yours, so there's a rumor that you've had a herd in these hills for a long time."

"Rolly." Canavan hesitated, then went on, "I've heard a rumor about another man who lives on the VV. When I was out there I saw a small cabin across the wash, and a trail of smoke from the chimney. Do you know anything about that?"

"No, I surely don't. All I know is that none of us, when I worked there, were allowed near that cabin. What about it, Mabry?"

"Same thing. Star used to go over there sometimes, but even Kerb Dahl acted funny about it. In all the fuss I'd sort of forgotten about it. In fact, we paid it no mind. In a case like that a body is right curious, but after a while he accepts it as one of the circumstances of the situation and pays it no mind."

Canavan considered the situation, running over all the details in his mind. He knew what he had to do. The big question was: would he last long enough to do it? Without a doubt Levitt would have a shoot-on-sight order for any of the three. It was the risk he must take, and the time to act was now.

When morning came to the hills again, Bill Canavan caught up the Appaloosa, then changed his mind and switched to one of the horses from the lava beds, a dun with black legs, mane and tail. That Appaloosa, he reflected, would be a dead giveaway . . . they would spot him a mile away on that horse.

He had ridden the dun several times, working cattle. It was a good, steady gelding with a good deal of cow sense and, mustang-bred, it was a good mountain horse. Not as fast as Rio, but a stayer.

He took a winding, roundabout route toward Soledad, one that kept him in the canyons and trees, out of sight of any chance watcher. It was a beautiful morning, the aspen leaves dancing lightly in the gentle wind, and a smell of pines and cedar on the wind. He drew up several times to look around, deliberately taking his time to enter town after darkness had fallen.

He was apprehensive. He had lived too long not to know the risk he took. Star Levitt needed him dead to complete the picture. He needed him dead and out of the way, and he would welcome this chance to get the job done before the outside law arrived.

From a mountain slope Canavan looked down on Soledad. That day, only weeks in the past, when he had ridden into the Valley like a conquering hero seemed long, long ago. He had believed he had planned for every eventuality, but so much else had intruded that only his basic plan remained, and at times he forgot that, worrying about Dixie.

The west was changing, and his very existence was evidence of it. He had lived through many phases of western life, but now he wanted to dig in, to settle down, to make a place for himself in the world. To become a citizen.

He smiled at his own thoughts, yet the smile faded. Why not? The country had needed discovery, had needed opening up. But now that was done and it was time to build. Many of the first ones had come to get rich and get out. But even they had served their purpose, for they pointed the way for others, helped to settle the land. And even many of those who wanted only riches had come to love the country and to stay.

Down there, its smoke lifting from its homes to the placid skies, lay Soledad. It was a simple little one-street town with a scattering of homes along shapeless avenues behind the facade of that one street, but a town of people. There were a lot of Anglo-Saxons down there, several Germans, a few Swedes and Nor-

wegians, one Jew and at least a dozen of the Irish.
There was also one Negro, a big, quiet man who ran
a saddlery and shoe shop combined. It was a western
town.

After visiting Soledad he would go to the VV,
and if she would come, he would bring Dixie away.
And at the same time he would check out that mys-
terious cabin that even Kerb Dahl seemed to fear.

The trail he had chosen was a trail he had
learned about from the same source who had told
him of the chance there might be cattle in the lava
beds, and of the secret trail to the mesa-top.

This might well be the last time he would need
such a trail. He could not hope to match Levitt in
numbers, but he might create some worry among his
followers—might even be able to contact the law.
That, if possible, he must do.

For some time he sat among the trees and looked
over the town. He was a good two miles off and
several hundred feet higher, so he had a first-class
view of all that went on. He could not, of course, dis-
tinguish one person from another, but he could see the
movement. And from his knowledge of the various
saloons, stores, and whatever, he could judge pretty
well what was happening.

There was no unusual activity. People seemed
to be going about their business as usual. Of course,
that was always true. One heard of gunfights in western towns, but they rarely touched the lives of the
average citizen. And many a man who lived in Dodge,
Deadwood or Tombstone never saw a gun fired in
anger.

Several times his eyes went to Scott's store. He
should talk to Scott. In many ways the old outlaw
puzzled him. He seemed settled and content . . .
But was he? Was he as much the innocent bystander
as he permitted people to believe? *"You're getting too
suspicious, Bill,"* he warned himself. *"Next thing you
know you'll be suspecting Dixie."*

He looked for Levitt's white horse, but saw it nowhere. The VV . . . He must circle around and have a look at the VV . . . And he might even see Dixie.

He went back to his horse and stepped into the saddle. Holding the reins, he looked once more at Soledad.

All was still . . . The smoke lifted lazily. A lone horseman trotted down the street. It was so very peaceful, so very still. Why then was he worried? Why was he apprehensive?

Was something wrong with him? Or was there something happening down there of which he knew nothing?

Chapter XIV

"There will be peace," Star Levitt said quietly, looking across the dining-room table at Dixie. "There will be peace in the Valley. No more killing, no more trouble. You and Tom here, you will have nothing to worry about."

Except being married to you! she said, mentally. *And what will happen to Bill?*

"Pogue and Reynolds were always fighting, and with them gone, things will settle down. It was fortunate that I got you away from there that day," he added. "The men were under some strain and there was considerable profanity, but I was afraid something might happen."

Afraid? Dixie asked herself. *Or did he know?*

Tom was quiet, his features cold and stiff, only his eyes seemed alive.

"I suspect," Levitt said, "that Canavan is dead.

I believe he was wounded in the branding-pen fight. He's not been seen since, and that's hardly like him.

"However, if he does show up, Marshal Chubb will be able to handle the situation. So you see, Dixie, you'll be marrying a pillar of the community." He smiled cynically. "I am sure the pillars of many other communities arrived at their positions in much the same way."

"It is the way of thieves," she said quietly, "to find excuses for their crimes. They always argue that everyone would steal if they had the chance. No doubt, some men have attained stature by devious means, but they are invariably found out."

He smiled. "You'd like to believe that, wouldn't you? But I'll not be found out, and soon the Valley will settle down and everyone will be pleased. Including me . . . And you.

"Oh, I know! You say you don't love me, but does it really matter? You'll live well, and you will soon forget there was any other way.

"Look around you." He gestured widely. "We're a little world of our own. The nearest other town is miles away. The people in authority in the Territory would rather not be bothered by our problems, if any. As soon as they are convinced all is well, they will go away and leave us in peace."

"You really think you're going to get away with it, don't you?" Tom Venable said. "You underrate Canavan. He will be back."

"I rather hope you are right," Levitt said, "for if he comes I shall have the pleasure of killing him." He paused. "And it will be a pleasure, I assure you."

There was a tap on the door, and Dixie, glad of the interruption, went to answer it.

Emmett Chubb stood in the doorway, hat in hand. "Boss," he paused. "Sorry to butt in, but there's some more of those cattle . . . the Gallow's Frame stock."

"What do you mean . . . *more?*" Levitt spoke irritably.

"Maybe fifty, sixty head. All big steers, prime stuff, all freshly branded."

"How fresh?"

"Two . . . three days, maybe. But wild and mean. I can't figure where they're coming from, Boss. It must be that Canavan . . . But where's he find them?"

"I think we'd better find out, Chubb. I'll leave that job to you . . . *Find out.*"

"What about town? Somebody'll have to be on duty in town?"

"Pick three good men, and let them look."

Chubb left and Levitt returned to the table, but his manner had changed. His desire to talk had disappeared, and he had the tight, mean look around his eyes that she was becoming used to. She shot a warning glance at Tom, and he nodded ever so slightly.

Levitt finished his meal in silence, emptied his cup and set it down hard on the table. He got up suddenly and started for the door, yet when he reached it, he turned sharply around. "I hope he's not dead! I want to kill him! I want to see him die!"

"Star," she spoke gently, "don't ever try it. He will kill you. He's too good for you, Star, and you know it!"

Had he been closer, he might have struck her. As it was he took an involuntary step back toward them, then paused, "I can beat him! I can beat anybody! Anyway," his manner calmed, "I've checked back on him. He's no gunfighter. He's used a gun a few times, that's all. He's nothing to worry about."

"Then stop worrying, Star." She smiled at him. "Kerb Dahl may get to him first . . . or Emmett Chubb."

When he was gone, Tom Venable looked at Dixie and shook his head. "Sis, be careful! He'll kill you, someday! I think he's a little mad, you know."

She nodded soberly. "You're right, of course,

but he rubs me the wrong way. And there's something about that inflated ego of his that makes me want to take him down a notch."

"I'm scared, Sis, really scared. Not for me so much as for you . . . for all of us. He *is* winning, you know."

She nodded. "I know. Tom, isn't there anything we can do?"

"He's too good with a gun. I've thought of that. Once I was even ready to shoot him in the back, but just as I put my hand on my gun I heard Dahl coming up behind me. 'You'd never make it,' was all he said. 'He'd kill you before you could draw.'

"I just stood there, half-scared at what I had almost done, and Dahl said, 'He's got a sixth sense, like eyes in the back of his head. I seen a man try to kill him once. Don't ever try it.'"

For a long time they sat silent, thinking, wishing, wondering what they could do. Around them now he had a half-dozen men . . . tough men, ready to kill either or both of them.

"Sis, do you think he's afraid of Canavan?"

She thought of that only for a minute, then she refused the idea. "No, he's not afraid of anything. But it bothers him, I think, because Canavan is not afraid of him."

"Where does he get the cattle?" Tom wondered. "How can cattle get to that size without being branded? For they are freshly-branded, every one. And where does he go when he isn't in Soledad? He disappears, you know . . . just drops out of sight."

Where was he now? And why did she feel about him as she did? There was excitement in him, and great strength. But it was something more, for when with him she felt at ease, relaxed, and at home. There was a calmness about him, a quiet assurance that was balm to her spirit. Was it only now that she could feel like that? Only now when she needed him so desperately? Or would it be always?

Yet somehow he was one with this land she had

come to love. He was as if born from the rock, from the tree-clad hills, and somehow she could not imagine him anywhere else but in this wild, western land.

"What do you think of him, Tom?"

She did not need to ask, for he had been thinking of him, too, sensing the attraction he had for his sister.

"He's a good man. A hard man, a lonely man, but a good man. I think, to use a term the cowhands use about some horses, he's a stayer. He wouldn't quit when the going got rough."

He stood up. "Dix, if you can get him, do it. You'll not find a better man."

He paused at the door to the inner room. "That depends, of course, on whether we get out of this alive . . . and whether he does."

The night was very still. There were lights in the bunkhouse but all else was quiet. The coals in the fireplace glowed red among the ashes. Another day without him, another day of trouble. How long could they stand it? How long could Tom stand it?

Levitt usually ignored Tom, but occasionally he seemed to try to goad him into some action. Of course, she admitted, Levitt's problems would decrease if Tom were dead. For the first time she looked at that aspect of it clearly, and the cold logic of it—as Levitt would see it—was simple indeed. In the event she married him, then his first action must be to eliminate Tom. No doubt Tom, being the cool head he was, already had come to that conclusion.

Levitt's marriage to her would give him a hold on the ranch. Tom's demise would tighten that control, and then, when he had tired of her . . . ?

She stood up, blew out the lamp, and went to bed.

Chapter XV

Circling Soledad again, Canavan came down through the pines and aspen to a position from which he could get a better view, and a view closer on, of the VV. Glass in hand, he took a comfortable position from which he could see all that transpired in the area below. Then he began a systematic study of the ranch and its environs.

The isolated cabin he located without trouble. He studied it for a long time, watching for any evidence of life, but he saw none. The place looked bare, lonely, abandoned. No smoke came from its chimney now, neither did anyone approach it. Obviously the cabin held someone or something of great importance to Levitt, or it would not be watched so closely. For it was watched.

There was somebody working near the stables who kept it in view. Yet after a careful study of the layout, Canavan decided the door of the cabin was actually not in view from the ranch house, for the view was cut off by the stable and several large stacks of hay.

As dusk drew on, he saw the man who had been working near the stable disappear, and Kerb Dahl appeared, wearing two guns.

As evening came, he saw Tom Venable come to the edge of the porch, look around and, after a few minutes, disappear within. Yet in that moment much had been obvious, for the instant Venable appeared in the door, Kerb Dahl had walked rapidly forward and stood in the middle of the yard facing him, for all the world like a prison guard.

The light of dusk faded and the stars appeared. There was a black bulge of cloud blotting out the stars over the mountains, however, and despite the pleasant evening here, there was a rumble of distant thunder. Was the storm approaching, or would it go around?

Aside from Kerb Dahl there was no evidence of life around the ranch—only the lights in the windows of the ranch house and occasionally a movement behind the curtains there. The white horse was saddled and standing at the corral bars.

How quiet it all seemed! And how peaceful! The elongated rectangles of light from the windows, the horses standing in the corrals, calmly eating hay, a dim light from the bunkhouse. Only the lonely, ominous figure in the yard—the man with the guns, watching.

Bill Canavan arose from his place and returned to his horse. He untied the dun, then stood for a moment, thinking. The feeling was on him of something about to happen, a restless, uneasy sense that worried him. He walked off, leading the horse.

He came off the ridge, concealed by the ridge itself, and came down into the sandy wash behind the ranch. There he stood for a long moment, listening. Then he led the horse up the wash until he was behind the stable, and in the deep shadows there he dropped the reins. The dun would not move from the place, as he had discovered ere this.

Loosening his guns in their holsters, he looked toward the isolated cabin. Then, taking a long breath, he went down into the gully and up to the house. It was dark enough now so his shadow would merge into that of the house. A man standing alone might be visible—certainly would be if he moved. But against the blackness of a building or a haystack, he could not be seen.

Stark and alone the little cabin stood on the knoll, a gloomy little building that seemed somehow ominous and strange. When alongside the building, he stopped and stood for a few minutes, listening for sounds from within. He heard nothing.

A low wind whispered around the eaves, and from the ranch house itself there came a rattle of dishes. The sound came clear on the cool night air. In the distance thunder rumbled again, and a wind skittered a few dry leaves across the hard ground. The only window in the cabin was curtained from within by what might be an old blanket. After a moment of waiting, he moved to the door.

His heart pounded against his ribs. He seemed to have trouble getting his breath. He took several long, even breaths to ease the tension and to prepare himself for whatever might come. Flattened against the building, he listened again . . . Nothing.

It was darker now, for the looming clouds were nearer. The rumble of thunder sounded like a gloomy lion, muttering in his cage. Canavan reached out and touched the doorknob. The metal felt strangely cold to his fingers, and with his right hand on his gun butt, he turned the knob. The door was locked.

Gently, he released the knob. The pause irritated him. He had built himself up for a crisis that now was frustrated in this most obvious of ways. The piling up of suspense made him reckless. A glance toward the ranch reassured him. There was no movement. Dahl must have gone inside for his slicker.

Here was a puzzle he must solve, and he probably would never have so good a chance again. Behind this locked door might lie the answer to many things. Certainly he must know, once and for all, what was here. If it was nothing, then at least one more item could be scratched. First, he must know. And the lonely cabin might be a death trap.

Light now streamed from the bunkhouse windows. The dim light previously seen might have come from a lamp with the wick turned low, yet now it was bright. Dahl might still be inside. Once there was a loud splash, as somebody threw some water from a basin to the ground outside. Taking the knob in his hand he turned it, then putting his shoulder to the door he braced his feet and pushed.

The construction was flimsy enough. The cabin was old, and whatever was here was evidently guarded well enough by Dahl and the others to keep it secure.

Canavan relaxed, took a deep breath, and pushed again. Something cracked sharply and instantly he drew back and flattened against the wall, his hand on his gun.

From within the cabin there was no sound. From the other buildings there was no unusual sound. He waited an instant, listening. Then, hearing nothing, he turned sharply around and put his shoulder to the door. It gave way so suddenly that he fell, catching himself on his hands and knees. He arose swiftly, gun in hand, but all was still. Whatever damage he had done to the door had been done before, and it had simply needed opening.

Eyes wide in the darkness, he peered around, trying to make out what the room contained, for it was simply one room and no more.

The door standing open let in a little gray light. As his eyes grew accustomed to the darkness, he could make out a chair lying on its side, a worn table with an empty basin, and a cot covered with rumpled bedding. Against the wall were several boxes, stacked in a neat pile. Nothing else seemed to offer anything.

Crossing to them, he hefted the top box. It was not heavy. Slipping the blade of his hunting knife under the thin slat that topped the box, he pried, ever so gently, not wishing to break his knife. The slat loosened and he dug his fingers into the crack. Risking the screech of a nail, he pulled up the slat. If there was any sound it was lost in a convenient rumble of thunder.

Inside the box there was sacking, and when that was parted, he found stacks of round cans, slightly larger but not unlike snuff cans. Lifting one to his nostrils, he sniffed curiously. From the box came a pungent, half-forgotten odor.

"So that's it?" he muttered. He frowned thoughtfully. It did not clarify the position of the Venables . . . although in some way, it might.

For a moment, he stared into the darkness. Dixie? He could not believe it. Nor Tom, when it came to that. Yet who was to know? Dark currents flow through the hearts of men, and even the seemingly most decent people sometimes—

No! That he could not believe! Not of either of them nor of Levitt, for that matter. He was, whatever else he might be, a strong man, strong-willed, and with nothing in the way of superficial weakness. His character was flawed, seriously flawed, but not in that direction.

Pocketing three of the small cans, he replaced the boards as best he could to conceal the most obvious damage. Then he slipped outside and pulled the door closed behind him.

Disturbed by the sudden turn of events, he went back to his horse. He stood there a moment, reassuring the animal that it was not abandoned. Then he went around the stable toward the house.

Nearby was a window, and he moved up under
the trees and hesitated there, taking stock. He should
get out now before he was discovered. But, on the
other hand, if he could see Dixie, if he could get her
to leave with him . . .

Eavesdropping was something he had no taste
for, but he had to know who was inside and what
was taking place. He hesitated only a moment longer,
then moved into the darkness close to the house and
to the side of the window.

It was the dining room of the small ranch house,
and three people sat at the table. Dixie was there,
looking pale but composed, and beside her, Tom
Venable. At the head of the table sat Star Levitt!

The window was opened slightly and he could
hear their voices. Levitt was speaking. "To me it is
the obvious solution, Dixie." His tone was suave, but
decisive. "We shall be married in this house on Monday. Do you understand?"

"You can't get away with this!" Tom said angrily,
but the undercurrent of hopelessness was obvious in
his tone. "It's the devil of a thing! Dixie hates you!
What sort of mind can you have?"

"Not your sort, evidently, Tom. There are different sorts of minds, you know. Some wish to have a
woman who loves them. That's nonsense, you know!
Much better to have a woman who hates you . . . de-
tests you. The very fact that you love a woman de-
prives you of the strength to deal with her. Love is
for peasants. I shall be much more amused by having
a woman who hates me, who would like to kill me!
Think of the man who handles tigers in a cage!
Handles them with a whip! That's the style."

"You're insane," Tom said.

Levitt shrugged. "Perhaps. There are many of us
about. You've read too many romances, Tom. Someday you will learn." He smiled. "In fact, if you
stay with us, I am sure you will learn."

He sipped his coffee. "It will be convenient to

be married to Dixie. Aside from the fact that she is very beautiful, very spirited and proud, there remains the fact that if anything ever did go wrong here, a wife cannot testify against her husband. With her as my wife I scarcely believe you'd ever care to bring any charges against me, Tom. But on the other hand, I mean to make this relationship very lucrative for you. I wouldn't want my brother-in-law to be a pauper, you know, so I shall see that you do very well." He smiled. "And become even more deeply involved. You can't blame a man for protecting himself."

"I've a damned good notion to—!" Tom half-rose from his chair.

"Have you, Tom? If I were you I'd make no trouble. None at all. You're in very deep, you know. Murder is a nasty charge, and now smuggling as well. Oh, yes! I've managed to arrange things so, if anything ever happens, it is you who have done all this." He waved a careless hand. "And there is evidence to prove it. Even if somehow you got out of the murder charge, there would still be enough to send you away for twenty years . . . And, although I should regret it, your sister, too. So I'd relax and enjoy things if I were you.

"Also, if you were exposed as operator of a ring of opium smugglers, think of the effect on your proud old father and his bad heart!"

"If it weren't for my father," Tom Venable said quietly, "I'd kill you with my bare hands!"

Levitt smiled. "I think not, Tom. I am several times stronger than you. I am stronger than anyone you have ever known or are likely to know. I've had a few fights, you know, if one wished to call them that. But so far I've never needed more than one hand."

"You know, Tom," Dixie's tone was casual, conversational. "I really believe we should talk this over between us. I am not at all sure that prison wouldn't be preferable to a marriage with Star Levitt."

Levitt's face was ugly. "You're flattering!" he commented dryly. "And not very appreciative. What would have happened to Tom had I not gotten him away from that mess and brought him here?

Canavan's ears missed a few words, but then Levitt went on, his tone a shade louder.

"Yes, I really believe I should have earned your gratitude. Instead I find you falling for an ordinary, drifting cowhand."

Dixie Venable's eyes lifted from her plate. "It does no good to tell you, Star. For with that vast ego of yours, you could never understand. But Bill Canavan, the drifting cowhand you speak of, is several times the man you could ever have been, even if you hadn't become a thief and a blackmailer of women!"

Canavan's heart gave a great leap, and in that instant he would cheerfully have gone right through the window, glass and all, and cheerfully given his life if it would have helped. Yet even in his elation at her praise of him he could not but admire her coolness and composure. Even in such a moment and in such a place, subject to any whim of the man across the table—a man who had already demonstrated his capacity for ruthlessness—she handled herself with courage. He stared into the window, his heart pounding. And just then she lifted her eyes and looked right into his!

For an instant that seemed an eternity, their eyes held. Then she turned her head, passing a dish to her brother with an idle comment that ignored Levitt completely.

When she spoke again her voice was a little louder, as if she wished for him to hear. "Well," she said, "everything is all right for the time being. At least, Star, you have given me until Monday!"

He drew back from the window. That message was for him, and between now and Monday was a lifetime . . . three whole days!

Three days in which much might be done, in

which he might somehow get her away from here—or in which he might kill Star Levitt.

Now, he knew that was what he would do if worst came to worst. Never yet had he actually hunted a man down to kill him. Nor had he ever set out to kill a man. He had killed, but only in defending himself or whatever or whoever it was he was protecting. He had never belted on a gun for the purpose of killing.

There had been times . . . He remembered that desperate moment on the old Butterfield stage when three men had suddenly leaped down in front of the stage and ordered the others to throw up their hands. The driver had made a move to quiet his team, and when he moved they shot him. In an instant, Canavan fired. He fired one barrel, then the other, and two men were on the ground. And he nailed the third with a pistol shot at eighty yards. Brought him down, at least. Two of the men lived to hang, and the day they were hung Canavan was driving stage in place of the man they had murdered . . . his shotgun beside him.

That had been long ago, and he never thought back to the moment. The time for action had come and he had not thought, but simply reacted as was necessary. And he had brought the stage and its passengers and shipments in safely.

It was time to leave. From the darkness under the trees he surveyed the ground he must cover. It was very dark now, with occasional flashes of lightning. He started for the stable and his horse and, just as he stepped past the last tree—a huge old cottonwood—a man stepped out of the darkness.

"Pete? Is that you? You got a match?"

It was Kerb Dahl!

Recognition came to them at the same instant, and Dahl let out a startled grunt and went for his gun.

There was no chance to grapple with the man,

no chance for a quick, soundless battle. Too much space intervened between them, and even as Dahl's hand closed over his gun butt, Canavan fired.

He had no recollection of drawing, no thought of it, he had needed the gun and had reacted instantly. Flame stabbed from the muzzle once, then again. Dahl took a hesitant step forward, his own gun belching flame through the bottom of its holster, and then he fell to his knees and pitched forward on his face. In that instant, the rain began to fall.

Then the bunkhouse door slammed open and somebody yelled, "Kerb! What's up? What's happened?"

Canavan rounded the stable, grabbed up the trailing bridle reins and swung to the saddle. The dun was no fool and took off from a stand into a dead run, running like a scared rabbit.

Behind him, somebody fired a futile shot, then another. But he was already out of sight in the darkness and the rain, and the dun was running all-out down the muddy trail. He held to the Soledad road for the sake of making time, and by the time he reached the outskirts of town there was no question of pursuit. He turned into the desert and wove his trail into that of some passing cattle. Then he fell into the trail left by the incoming stage and from it took to the alleyways and byways of town—avoiding the streets, where he might be seen.

He had no intention of stopping in Soledad, only losing his trail there, for he circled through the town and picked up the trail to Thousand Springs Mesa.

He patted the dun on the shoulder. "Good boy! You saved my bacon tonight!"

Pausing on the trail, he took time to dig his slicker out of the roll behind the saddle, and slipped into it. Lightning flashed, thunder rolled, and the rain came down in torrents. He swore softly, not bitterly, and rode on. "God have pity on the poor sailors on such a night as this!" he said, and rode on into the night.

What was all that about a murder charge against Tom Venable? And what was their connection to the smuggling of opium? He had recognized the smell the instant he sniffed the can. It was an odor one did not soon forget, and he had smelled it first in a joint on the Barbary Coast.

Now he must think; he must plan. Somehow he had to free Dixie from this entanglement, and if there was no other way, he would face Star Levitt with a gun.

Yet it was not the way he wanted it. There had to be a better way.

Chapter XVI

Bill Canavan's course lay clear before him. All other plans must be shelved, so that the whole situation could be brought into the open by Monday. Whatever else needed to be done must now wait until another time.

He was under no illusions. He had killed Kerb Dahl. And Dahl was one of their warriors, a man upon whom they depended much—and the strong right hand of Star Levitt. His victory had been a shock to Canavan.

He had always been good with guns. He was an instinctively good shot, pointing the gun as one would a finger. And he had always hit what he shot at. Yet he had never thought of himself as a gunfighter, nor in the same class with those who had won notoriety in that field.

With an even break he had beaten Kerb Dahl, and by a good margin.

It meant only one thing to Bill Canavan. He might survive. He had never really given himself much of a chance, for although he knew he had the courage to face a gun—something he had done in the past—he had never considered himself good enough to win.

His only chance was, however, to meet the investigating officers, whoever they might be, and state his case. Otherwise he would simply be declared an outlaw.

Canavan was fully aware that Levitt planned to give him no such chance.

There was little talk beside the fire on the mesa that night. He explained simply what had happened, and Burt looked at him thoughtfully. "If you beat Dahl you must be pretty good."

"It was an even break, although I was all keyed up for it. Maybe that gave me the edge."

He was tired. He realized that more tonight than ever before. He seemed to have been doing nothing but riding and watching, always alert for trouble, always knowing it was out there waiting for him.

It was scarcely seven o'clock when he stretched out under the stars. He remembered looking up at them and wondering where the clouds had gone, then recalling that the storm had not come this far north.

He awakened in the cool dawn with a blush of pink upon the lava beds. And he lay for a while watching the light change on the clouds.

Rolly Burt was already up, and he could smell wood smoke and hear the faint crackle of the flames, for the fire was small. He sat up at last and put on his hat. Then he threw the blankets back and got up, pulling on his pants and shaking out his boots. This morning he had collected nothing but a half-grown tarantula, who reared up menacingly. But Canavan was in no mood for trouble, and the big spider wandered away to come again another night. He hadn't been looking for trouble, anyway, just a warm place to sleep. And that big thing, whatever it was, had no right to shake him out of his bed at such an ungodly hour.

Canavan walked to the spring and, kneeling beside the pool below it, he splashed water on his face and neck and washed his hands with the soap Burt had left there. Using the pool for a mirror, he combed his hair with a broken bit of comb.

Burt looked up. "If you figure to go courtin'," he said, "you'd better stand close to a razor."

Canavan felt of his jaws. "Wasn't countin' on it, to tell the truth. But maybe if I'm going to talk to some judge or sheriff from back in God's country, I'd better shave up a mite."

"You say he sent for the law?"

"Sure. He's no damn fool. If he can bring them in here and get a clean bill, then we become outlaws and he comes out smelling like a rose."

"County seat is over a hundred miles by trail," Mabry commented. "If he gives them an idea the situation is under control, they'll be only too glad to go home and forget about it. I been four, five years in this country an' never seen no kind of an officer.

"Year or two afore I come in, there was a deputy sheriff rode in here and somebody shot him. They dropped his star back at the county seat an' that's the last officer we've had up here until now."

"At least," Burt said, "the last one would admit to it."

Mabry glanced at him, but offered no comment.

On Sunday night they rode to Soledad, three strong young men who knew where they rode and what the consequences might be. They rode because of loyalty to one another, because the ranches for which they had worked had suffered, and because a woman was in trouble. They also rode because in each of them there was a sense of what was right and what was justice, although none of them would have admitted to it or would have known how to phrase it.

They had never learned how to rationalize, and

their world was a simple one where right and wrong were quite obvious.

Bill Canavan pondered grimly upon his own fortunes—or lack of them. He had come to Soledad a soldier of fortune, riding to the conquest of a disputed valley. And he had remained to find himself fighting a lonely battle for what seemed a lost cause.

His own fortunes were scarcely to be considered now. He hardly remembered the water rights he held. His one thought now was to free Dixie from whatever entanglement she was in . . . Whatever else happened was beside the point.

Yet in the minds of all was another thing. For they all remembered the thunder and flash of the guns that mowed down friends or acquaintances, that killed good, hard-working men because they stood in the way of Star Levitt.

They drew up on the outskirts of town. "It looks quiet enough, but I'd suggest you leave your horses at May's. Put them out of sight in the stable and I'll leave mine there, too. Be ready to run. We may have to make a break for it. And it will be every man for himself, if we can get away, or else none of us may make it. You boys can hide out in May's stable, if you want, or try to see Kinney.

"I shall go right to Scott. He can get hold of Allen for me if you boys haven't seen him. Keep out of sight. If the worst comes, I'll go gunning for Star. I never went after a man yet, but rather than see him force Dixie into marriage, and win out here after all he's done, I'll do it."

"Who are those gents Levitt sent for?" asked Burt.

"Look, he knew some word of this would get out . . . It always does. So he wrote to the governor and to the sheriff as well. He wants the whole thing cleared up, and the blame put where it should be. Of course, he has his trail covered, and he knows they'll end up blaming the Pogue-Reynolds feud.

"Levitt will do most of the talking, and the witnesses he brings in will agree with what he's said. Then the affair will be smoothed over and he will be seen by them to be a stable, honest citizen."

"Looks like he's drawin' to a pat hand. How d' you figure we have a chance?" said Mabry.

"Well, I want to get to the official, whoever he is, and tell our story before Levitt can. I'm holding the joker in the deck, but of course Levitt doesn't know that."

"What is this here joker?"

"Wait. We'll keep that for the showdown."

He led off, walking the Appaloosa through the encircling trees to May Ashton's place on the outer fringe of Soledad. There was no one in sight, but a lamp was alight inside the cabin, and the one window that opened toward the barn and the corral showed a thread of light below the curtain.

Canavan took his horse inside and tied him in a stall, forked some hay into the manger and left the others to do likewise.

Slipping along the wall he glanced into the window and saw her there, sewing by lamplight. She seemed to be alone.

She opened the door at his tap and he stepped inside. She closed the door behind him. "I'm glad you've come," she said. "Allen was wondering how he could get word to you. Dixie is to be married tomorrow."

"I know. How about the officers from the capital? Have they come?"

"They're supposed to be here in the morning. The sheriff is coming from the county seat, and some attorney from the capital will be here to represent the governor. Two state Rangers are coming with them. I've heard it all being discussed in the restaurant, although most of those I've heard speak of it want nothing to do with any of them. They're afraid."

"Can't say I blame them. Has there been any talk about a hearing?"

"They will hold it in the lobby of the Cattleman's Hotel. It's the only place large enough, aside from the Bit and Bridle. That man Voyle was talking to Syd Berdue about it."

She paused. "Bill, there's one thing you should know. There's a warrant out for your arrest. They want you for killing Kerb Dahl. Was it you?"

"Yes. But it was a fair fight. In fact, he went for his gun first. I had no choice but to shoot."

"There's a question there, Bill. Please think of it. Levitt says you were a prowler, and Dahl was only protecting the ranch."

"What does Dixie Venable say? It is her property, after all."

"She won't say anything. I don't know why, but I know she will not. And don't expect anything from her."

She filled a cup of tea. "It's not coffee. I drink tea here at home."

"No problem. My mother used to drink it. She drank green tea, though."

"That's what this is."

She sat down across the table from him. "Bill, they have a reward for you . . . dead or alive. An even thousand dollars."

He whistled. "That's enough to get the bounty hunters out. Now listen: I am going to see Scott . . . I know, you weren't aware that I knew him, but I do. He's a friend . . . or I think he is.

"Mabry and Burt are both in town. Burt limps a little, but he can get around. They'll hide out either in your stable or in the woods close by in case of an emergency. If I get into trouble I'll try to get word to you, and you can pass it along to them.

"If the worst comes to the worst, I'll try to give myself up to the state officials and try to get an im-

mediate hearing. Due to the fact they've come so
far to investigate, I don't think they'll argue that. Then
at least I can get the facts before them."

"Bill, don't count on anybody siding with you.
Chubb has been around town with Hanson, dropping
hints of what might happen to anyone who helped you
in any way. You can't depend on any of them. I'm not
even sure I'd help if it wasn't for Allen Kinney. But
he's in it with you, of his own free will.

"They've all got the example of what happened at
the branding pens to show them how ruthless Levitt
is. He smiles very pleasantly and comments on how
awful it was, and how you must have been the in-
stigator of it."

The street was dark when he left May's, and he
did not try to hide but walked off up the street as
any casual stroller might. To try to slink along would
immediately excite suspicion if he was seen.

Old Man Scott was the one he must see, and he
must get to him at once. Scott would know what
it was best to do, and Scott would know how to get
in touch with the state officers. Also, his place would
be a good place to keep out of sight and still have a
listening post where he could know all that transpired in the town.

A half-dozen horses were tied in front of the Bit
and Bridle. There was light flooding from the windows, and a sound of loud talk and laughter from
within.

A man opened the door and stumbled into the
street, and for an instant Canavan hesitated, suddenly
uneasy. The street was altogether too quiet, and there
was too little movement. Turning at right angles, he
went between two buildings, heading for the back
door of Scott's place.

He thought he detected a movement in the shadows and, pausing, he held still for a count of six. Nothing moved. Seeing nothing more, he went to the back

door of Scott's place and tapped lightly. The door opened and he stepped in.

Scott stepped back, alarm in his eyes. "Man, you've stirred up a peck o' trouble! You've got the whole country stood on its ear."

He filled a cup with coffee and put it on the table in front of Canavan. "Drink that. Make you feel better."

"Thanks." He looked up at Scott again. Was it his imagination or was the old man acting different than he would have expected? Was this whole affair making him unreasonably suspicious?

"Big trouble's busting loose," Canavan said, "I hope I can handle it. Scott, you've got to help me get in touch with those state officers when they arrive. I've got to see them right away."

His ears caught a faint whisper of movement outside, and the cup stopped halfway to his lips. He looked up at Scott and felt something turn sick inside him.

Old Man Scott held a shotgun in both hands, the twin barrels pointed right at his chest. "You just sit tight, son, an' you won't get killed. You just do like I say." He raised his voice. "You make a wrong move an' I'll cut you in two!"

He spoke even louder. "All right, out there! I've got him! You can come in now!"

The door burst open and Voyle was the first man in, with Allen Kinney right behind him, then Tolman and Emmett Chubb.

Chubb's satisfaction was obvious. "Well, Canavan! Who's top-dog now?" He lifted his pistol.

"Hold it!" Scott's shotgun made a sharp movement. "Just take her easy there, Chubb! This man's my prisoner. I'm claimin' the reward right now! Moreover, I'm holdin' him alive for Mr. Levitt!"

"Like hell!" Chubb declared. "The orders are to shoot on sight!"

"Not unless you want a blast from this shotgun!" Scott said. "Nobody's beatin' me out of my money! This feller Kinney has a finger on a piece of it, I reckon, but nobody else! Kinney tipped me off, but nobody else gets a hand on that money but us!"

Baffled, Chubb hesitated, wanting to shoot but not liking to take a chance against a shotgun at that range.

Scott was a tough old man and would very likely do just as he threatened.

"He's right, Emmett," Kinney said. "He got him first."

Bill Canavan stared from one to the other. "Sold out!" he sneered. "I might have suspected it!"

Kinney flushed, but Scott shrugged. "A thousand dollars is a lot of money, boy! And they were goin' to get you anyway! I've seen men killed for a sight less, and most of these folks around here would have killed you. They'd have taken a shot at you and talked about it after!"

"We'll take him to jail then!" Chubb said. "This is no place for him."

"You'll do no such thing!" Scott said. "He stays right here until I have the money right in my hand! When Levitt's paid me, he can do whatever he's of a mind to, but nobody's beatin' me out of my money! Stay here and help guard if you want, but don't you forget for one minute that he's my prisoner! This shotgun won't forget it!"

Kinney slipped around behind Canavan and lifted his guns from their holsters. Reluctantly, under the pointing shotgun, Canavan backed into a chair and sat down. Shocked by the unexpected betrayal, he could only stare accusingly, appalled by the sudden turn of fortune.

From the high, if desperate, hopes of earlier in the day, he was suddenly thrust back into utter hopelessness. Yet he was alive, and had Scott yielded him to Chubb he would never have lived to reach the jail.

How could they have known he was even in town? There was but one way . . . May must have betrayed him. She and Allen must have planned it together, and when he left her house she must have gotten the word to Kinney at once.

He sat very still, thinking. There had to be a way out. There was always a way, if one could but think of it, and there was no need to waste time in wailing at the fact that he had been betrayed or that he was now a prisoner. The problem he must solve was what was now to be done.

What was past was past. He had only to do with the future. Fortunately, Scott had insisted he be held here, so he would not be murdered en route to the jail.

Chubb dropped into a chair opposite him and held a six-shooter in his lap. "I'd like to blast his heart out," he said sullenly. "What frets you so much, Scott? You'll get your money, dead or alive."

"You just leave him be," Scott said. "If you shoot him, you'll lay claim to it. I wouldn't trust you across the street where that much money was concerned. Nor any of your crowd!"

He chuckled, avoiding Canavan's eyes. "Levitt will be top man around here from now on, and he's the one I'll do business with—and only with him! I'm too old to be shoved out in the cold at my time of life, and I ain't figurin' on it! I'll work with Star an' he'll work with me!"

"I never saw you bein' so thick with him!" Chubb argued, his irritation obvious. "I never even seen him in your store."

Scott chuckled. "How d' you suppose he came here in the first place? Who told him this place was wide open for a smart man?

"Canavan here, he figured the same way. He

planned to take over when Pogue and Reynolds were out of it, but he was leavin' too much to chance. Star Levitt doesn't leave anything to chance."

Bitterly, Bill Canavan stared at the floor, trying to shut out their words. All he wanted was time to think. Otherwise he was finished, really finished . . . And so were Dixie and Tom Venable.

If Mabry and Burt had gone to May's, or had stayed there after stabling their horses, they would have been sold out, too. He listened, straining his ears to catch any distant sound of shooting, but heard nothing. By now both might be dead, led into a trap by him.

Levitt was completely in command now. These others were aware of that and all were jumping on the bandwagon to ride home with the winner. He stared at Kinney, and the young man's eyes wavered and swung away from his. How could he have guessed such a man would sell him out? He would have bet his life on him . . . And that was just what he had done . . . and lost.

As for Scott, the old man had been an outlaw most of his life. When a man rides on the wrong side of the law for so long, he can develop a bent that way. Still, the friends who directed Canavan to him had always said he was a man to ride the river with. But who was he to ride with?

The old man had evidently chosen to ride with the front-runner as he had said, and it was certainly the logical thing to do. Yet he had liked the old man, felt a genuine affection for him. Which only went to prove that one should never let sentiment involve one's judgment.

There was no chance now for Dixie, unless . . . His eyes narrowed with thought.

What would they do with him now? Would they get word to Star that he was a prisoner, then smuggle him out of town to be killed? Or would they bring him out in the open with the evidence arrayed against him, or kill him trying to escape?

If, somehow, he could manage to talk to Ward Clymer or the sheriff! Of course, he would be meeting them with reward posters out on him, with all of Levitt's men prepared to swear to his crimes, and he would be in a bad position to begin with. And what evidence had he?

On his part, Star Levitt would have plenty of evidence arranged for, and more than enough perjured testimony. And, as May had warned him, nobody in town would testify against Star.

They were frightened, or they wanted to ride with the front-runner.

He was through . . . finished.

Yet . . . there was a slim hope. Mabry and Burt had not been brought in yet, and he had heard no report of their deaths. Their names had not even been mentioned thus far, so perhaps they had not been taken. And they, at least, were loyal. Somehow, if they were still alive and free, they would try to help. Somehow they would contrive to free him.

It was going to be a long night, and a longer day tomorrow.

And tomorrow was Dixie's wedding day. . . .

Chapter XVII

The night was endless, and the darkness lasted forever. In the back room of Scott's store, lighted by the small flame of but one coal-oil lamp turned low, they sat in silence, watching the minutes become hours. And for a long, long time it seemed there would be no day.

Scott smoked endlessly at the stub of a cigar that seemed never to have been longer, and seemed never to grow shorter. Chubb smoked cigarettes, pacing the floor, occasionally swearing, turning his head as a lizard does to stare unblinking at Canavan. Allen Kinney read from a week-old newspaper only just arrived. Voyle yawned, dozed, occasionally smoked.

"If you'd let me have him," Chubb complained, "we could all get some sleep."

"No," Scott said.

The door from the back room opened into the store, and beyond it they could see the street. And for a long time it was only blackness there, then a faint gray, and finally they could pick out the astonished eyes of the stores across the street.

"You'll die this day," Chubb said, with satisfaction.

"Maybe," Canavan replied, "but have you looked in a mirror this morning?"

"Mirror?" Chubb turned on him. "Why should I?"

"Because you've the mark of death on you, Chubb. You'll not live out the day, I'm thinking, and —" he began his lie, "I'm the seventh son of a seventh son, and can see the future. If I were you, I'd make my peace with the Lord."

"You're crazy!" Chubb turned away. But a moment later they saw him looking into Scott's shaving mirror.

"The mark of death," Canavan said solemnly. "You might live out the day, but they rarely do."

The room was silent. Voyle gnawed uneasily at his lower lip. In the street a Mexican went slowly past leading a burro piled high with sticks. An old gray mongrel trotted beside them.

Chubb looked at him. "You're crazy," he said. "All that stuff about seventh sons. That's nonsense."

"Is it? My uncle foretold his own death. To the minute. Told us he'd die by drowning and everybody laughed, because he was the strongest swimmer anywhere around. And besides, he was going into the desert for two weeks."

"So what happened?" Scott asked.

"He died by drowning . . . flash flood. His head struck on a stone when the wall of water hit him. He was drowned."

"Could happen to anyone," Voyle declared.

"It could," Canavan admitted. "But my uncle foresaw it, just like I'll foresee yours. The exact way hasn't come to me yet, but it will."

Chubb snorted his disgust. "You tell me when

you get the rest of it," he said. "Give me somethin' to laugh about."

"That's another thing," Canavan said quietly. "You're not going to laugh anymore, never any more at all!"

They heard the door slam over at the Bit and Bridle, and Pat stood on the walk, taking the morning air. Down the street a pump rattled, then broke into a rhythmical squeaking. Water gushed into the pail, and they all heard it. Canavan looked over at Scott, but the old man avoided his glance. For a moment Canavan was about to say something sarcastic, but then he figured, *what the hell?*

His lids fluttered, then closed. Yet behind them he was thinking. With four of them watching he had no chance, none at all.

In a few minutes, at least within the hour, allowing for bad roads, the stage would roll into the street bringing the men from the capital. The stage would halt in front of the Cattleman's Café and the passengers would go inside to eat. Within a short time after they arrived he would know his fate . . . if Levitt did not come first.

"Al," Scott said suddenly, "you take this shotgun, and I'll assemble some ham an' eggs for you boys. No reason to go hungry."

Tolman, who had left some time before, returned now and stuck his head into the door. "Stage a-comin' an' Syd Berdue just blowed in!"

"The VV outfit come in yet?" Chubb asked, without turning his eyes from Canavan. "When Dolph Turner comes in, tell him what's happened. He'll see that Levitt gets the news right off!"

Scott was working over the stove, and soon the smell of frying bacon and eggs filled the room. Despite his situation Canavan realized suddenly that he was hungry, very hungry indeed. He realized for the first time that he had eaten nothing the night before.

Emmett Chubb rose and crossed the room to

wash his face and hands. He was a stocky, swarthy man with a square jaw and a dark stubble of beard. His hair was unkempt, and Canavan noted the notches on his guns. Three on one, five on the other. The notches stamped the man, for only tinhorns notched their guns as a rule. Eight men dead . . . It was time for *him* to die.

"The only thing I'm sorry for," Chubb said, as he dried his hands, "is that we didn't get a chance to settle this between us."

His black eyes were hard as agate. "I'd like to see you down in the dust, Canavan. I'd like to see you die."

"We could do it now," Canavan suggested. "Just give me a gun and we can step right out there. I wouldn't have to worry because I know you're not going to make it. Your number's up."

"Stow that!" Chubb said carelessly, but Canavan could see Chubb was nettled by it. No man likes to be told he is about to die, and especially not a man who may have to use a gun at any moment.

"All of you," Canavan continued, "are a bunch of yellow-bellied double-crossers. There isn't one of you fit to stand up with a man.

"As for facing me, Chubb," he said cooly, "you had your chance after you murdered Vin Carter. You blew town almighty fast so you wouldn't have to answer for it. You put your tail between your legs and ran." He spoke softly, bitterly. "I'd lay a little money that every one of those eight notches was for some helpless drunk. I don't think you've got the guts to face a sober man, Chubb. I think you're yellow!"

Chubb strode across the room and slapped Canavan across the face. And Canavan came up from his chair with a lunge.

"Stop it." Kinney yelled. "Damn you, Chubb! Just back up now! Back up and sit down or you'll die right here!"

Chubb backed away warily, not liking the expression in Kinney's eyes. "Hold it now, you just hold it. He's got no call to—"

Suddenly the door opened and three men pushed into the room. Bill Canavan saw that Star Levitt was the first man into the room, and something went cold and still within him. The next two men were strangers.

Levitt glanced quickly from Scott to Chubb, then indicated the two men with him. "Neal and Baker of the Rangers. They will take charge of the prisoner."

Chubb swore, disappointment and resentment struggling for place in his eyes. "He's here. We've been holdin' him."

"*I've* been holding him," Scott said. "Me an' Kinney here. Chubb had nothin' to do with it."

Neal gestured to Canavan. "You come with us. We're holding a hearing right now. We want to find out just what has happened here, and why."

Canavan started for the door with Neal, and as he glanced back he saw Scott smiling. And as their eyes met the old man winked.

Now what did that mean? Frowning, Canavan walked across the street toward the hotel. Neal glanced at him several times. "Do you know a man named Mabry?"

"I know him. He works for me, and he's a good man. Is he all right?"

"When Clymer asks you questions," Neal said, "just give him what information you have—straightforward, honest and without prejudice."

Puzzled by the suggestion, Bill Canavan walked into the room and was shown to a chair.

A big man sat at a table in front of the room. He had a strong, capable look about him, and as Canavan came in he glanced at him sharply, then returned to the documents on the table before him. Several others entered, and among them were Dixie and Tom Venable. More and more puzzled, he glanced from one to the other, trying to get some hint as to what had been happening—and what was to happen here.

Canavan had never believed that Levitt would permit Clymer to confront the Venables, nor himself if it could be avoided. Yet all were present, and it looked like a showdown. Allen Kinney came in with May. When she glanced at Canavan, he averted his eyes. Scott walked in, and then Star Levitt with Chubb and Voyle.

From the expression on Levitt's face, he had an idea all was not going to suit him. And the thought cheered him. Anything that was bad news for Levitt was apt to be good news for him.

Ward Clymer sat back in his chair and glanced around the room, his expression noncommittal. "Now, my friends," he began briskly, "this is an entirely informal hearing to try to clarify the events leading up to and subsequent to the gun battle in which Pogue and Reynolds were killed, and to try to ascertain the guilt, if any.

"Although your statements will be taken down in writing, you will not be sworn in at this time. But please remember that you may be called upon to repeat your statements under oath and before a jury.

"Also, I am given to understand that William Canavan, a cattleman, is being held on a charge of killing Kerb Dahl, a cowhand from the VV. If such proves to be the truth, and if the evidence warrants it, Canavan will be taken to the county seat for trial. In the meantime, let us have your statements and any information calculated to clarify the situation."

He glanced at Star Levitt. "Mr. Levitt, will you relate the events that preceded the fight between Reynolds and Pogue?"

Star Levitt got to his feet. He glanced around, smiled a little, and began. "From what I have heard, it seems that for some time before I came into the Valley there had been trouble between the two outfits, with sporadic trouble over water and range rights.

"The VV, owned by the Venables, was not involved in this feud, but there seemed to be some desire on the part of both outfits to possess the VV holdings and their water.

"As you will understand, in any such semi-desert
range as this, water is the important factor. And who
controls the water controls the range, for without
water the range is useless.

"On the day of the big fight there had been some
minor altercation over branding. And it led to shooting,
which soon became general until most of the hands on
both sides were involved with the resulting deaths."

"You had no part in this fight?" Clymer asked.

"None. When trouble seemed about to develop,
I withdrew my men and got out of the way myself.
After the shooting was over we did what we could
for the wounded."

"Are there witnesses present from the outfits involved?"

"Yes, sir. Emmett Chubb, who has been the acting marshal, survived the fight. So did Voyle, of the
Box N. Kerb Dahl, of the VV, who was later murdered
by Canavan, was in the middle of things when it
happened."

"Sir?" Canavan asked suddenly.

Clymer's eyes shifted to him. "Did you have a
question?"

"Yes, sir. I'd like to ask Star Levitt what his range
holdings were."

"I fail to see that the question has any bearing
on the matter," Levitt replied cooly.

"It's a fair question and one we'd like to have
answered, as it may have a bearing on subsequent
testimony. Were you running cattle? And where was
your headquarters?"

Levitt hesitated, then said, "My headquarters
was on the VV. You see, I am soon to marry Dixie
Venable."

Clymer glanced curiously at Canavan. "Does that answer your question?"

"It is sufficient for the time. However, I'd like it to be plain to everybody that Star Levitt had no holdings in this Valley."

Levitt shrugged, and the attorney then asked Chubb and Voyle a few questions about the shooting at the branding pens. And through Scott and Pat, he brought out the facts of the longstanding feud between the two cattlemen. Every story seemed to bolster Levitt's position. Tom Venable told what he knew in brief, clipped sentences, offering nothing but replies to the direct questions.

Dixie was next, and her testimony was equally simple. As she started to return to her chair, Canavan spoke up. "Another question, Miss Venable. Did anyone warn you away from the roundup, advising you that there might be trouble?"

She paused only an instant. "Why, yes. Star Levitt did."

"I could see some of the men were spoiling for a fight," Star agreed calmly. "It seemed a bad place for a woman. Also, there was some rather profane language being used in the heat of the roundup."

"May I ask a few questions?" Canavan asked.

Levitt interrupted impatiently. "Mr. Clymer, this man Canavan is a trouble-maker! His questions can do no good except to put others in a bad light. The man is a murderer."

Clymer shook his head. "We shall deny no man a right to defend himself, Mr. Levitt. We are here only to ascertain the facts. Moreover, we must examine the prisoner in connection with the killing of Kerb Dahl. What have you to say to that, Canavan?"

"I should welcome an inquiry into the matter, sir. However, it is impossible to form a judgment without considering what happened before that shooting took place."

"That's reasonable enough," Clymer said. "Go ahead."

Levitt's lips tightened and his nostrils flared with anger. Voyle had come into the back of the room with Syd Berdue and they stood there, surveying the crowd. With them was the silent man who seemed to be Dahl's partner.

"I just want to ask Mr. Levitt how many cowhands he had when he rode into this country," Canavan suggested mildly.

Star was puzzled, but wary. "What difference does it make?"

"Please answer the question, Mr. Levitt," Clymer suggested. "We are simply trying to arrive at the facts, and if the matter can be settled here it will save us all a lot of trouble."

"How many hands, Levitt? You used the VV spread but how many hands did *you* have?"

"Why only one man actually came to the Valley with me," Levitt said. The question puzzled him, and what puzzled him disturbed him.

"That one man was the short, dark man now standing at the back of the room, wasn't it? The man called Turner?"

"That's right."

Canavan turned suddenly in his chair, to face Dahl's partner. "Turner, what's a piggin string?"

"What?" Turner was startled. He started to speak, then stopped, irritated at the sudden attention and a little frightened.

"I asked what a piggin string was?"

Turner glanced from one side to the other, as if seeking a way out. He wet his lips. Then shrugged. "I don't know. What difference does it make?"

"This makes no sense at all!" Levitt protested. "Let's get on with the hearing!"

"Turner, what's a *grulla?*"

"Lay off," Turner said angrily. "I've no part in all this!"

Canavan turned back to Clymer. "You, sir, were brought up on a cow ranch, or so I hear. You know that a piggin string is a short piece of rope or rawhide used to tie a crittur's legs when it's been thrown. You also know that a grulla is a kind of mouse-colored horse, usually a mustang.

"The point I'm getting at, and maybe I haven't made it too well, is that Levitt came into this country with one man who wasn't a cowhand. Turner doesn't know the first thing about a ranch or about cattle, except what he might have picked up since he came to this Valley."

"What's that got to do with it?" Levitt demanded.

Clymer was sitting back in his chair, obviously enjoying the discussion. He began to smile as if he anticipated the reply and the next question.

"Why, just this, Levitt. I'm right curious as to how many head of cattle you brought into the Valley, and how many head you have now."

Somebody out in the room grunted, and Scott was smiling. The question caught Levitt flat-footed, and Clymer sensed it. "That's a very good question, Mr. Levitt. On the way over here you told me you ran about a thousand head. Where did you get them?"

Levitt held himself very still, thinking rapidly and cursing himself for bragging to Clymer. He had thought to give him the opinion that he, Levitt, was a substantial citizen, based on the idea that the law was not prepared to suspect a rich man—or to move against him even if he was suspected.

"This is getting far from the subject," he replied cooly. "We actually came here to investigate a murder, committed by Canavan here. Now it begins to appear that I am on trial, not the murderer."

"On the contrary, Mr. Levitt, we came down here to investigate a multiple shooting, and the events that led to it, and to try to put a stop to what might develop as a result. The shooting of Kerb Dahl, as Canavan so rightly suggests, is only one aspect of it."

"I believe the question I have asked," Canavan said quietly, "must be asked. Before we can arrive at any conclusions, we must know what the issues are.

"Mr. Levitt here admits arriving in the country with only one man, one who is not a cowhand. No two such men could bring a thousand head of cattle into this or any other valley.

"However, I believe Levitt does have many cattle under his brand, and every brand has been worked over."

"That's a lie!" Levitt protested.

Canavan settled back in his chair. "Now ask me about the killing of Kerb Dahl," he suggested.

Star Levitt fought back his fury. This was a situation he had never wanted to develop. He had not planned it this way. It had seemed a simple task to bring the law to the Valley. And then, with the shooting of Dahl to build around, to incriminate Canavan, clearing himself and his men and then remaining in possession of the best ranch land in the Valley.

Invited to question Canavan about the shooting, he leaped at the opportunity. But before he could phrase his first question, Clymer interrupted. "Canavan, if, as you suggest, Mr. Levitt has many mis-branded cattle, and you maintain that neither he nor Turner are cattlemen, who did the branding?"

"Kerb Dahl, the man with whom I had the gun-fight on the VV, Voyle of the Box N, Tolman who was hired by Levitt, and Emmett Chubb, among others."

"That's absurd!" Levitt protested contemptuously.

Canavan turned to look at Dixie for the first time. "Miss Venable, will you name the men who met at Thousand Springs?"

The question caught her by surprise. Dixie glanced at him and her eyes wavered. Of course, she had no idea she had been observed. And before Levitt could catch her eye she said, "Why, Dahl was there, and Voyle, Tolman and Syd Berdue."

"What did they talk about?"

Levitt was straining forward in his chair, his eyes upon her. Dixie glanced at him, and her eyes wavered. "Why, I—" Her voice trailed off.

"Before you answer," Canavan said quietly, "let me tell you that you and your brother have been the victims of one of the foulest tricks ever played. And this is your time to become free again."

Canavan turned to Clymer. "Sir, Miss Venable was concealed near the Springs and overheard some conversation between the men mentioned. These were the same men who altered the brands for Levitt. Through them, Levitt engineered and planned the fight between the two major outfits, forcing the issue between Pogue and Reynolds. In that battle he arranged to have the two men who would oppose him in his takeover of the Valley ranches. It will no doubt strike you that among the survivors of the fight at the branding pens were *all* the men seen at the Springs by Miss Venable. And also seen by myself, incidentally.

"Also," he added, "Levitt was blackmailing the Venables, using their ranch as a storage depot and transfer point for his opium trade."

Levitt half-started to his feet, then sat down. His face showed the shock of the sudden exposure, but he was thinking swiftly, trying to find the right words to answer the charges and to turn them against Canavan. He still could not believe his plans had gone awry, that all his months of scheming and working and moving his men like pawns on a chessboard had been for nothing.

Canavan came to his feet, his ringing voice reducing to silence the sudden stir in the room. "Furthermore, I think this is the proper time to make certain other points clear." Opening his shirt he drew a leather wallet from inside it, and from the wallet took a handful of papers which he passed to Clymer. "Will you tell Mr. Levitt," he said, "what you have here?"

Clymer glanced at the papers, then looked up astonished. "Why, these are deeds!" he exclaimed, glancing from Canavan to Levitt. "These indicate that Mr. Canavan is the owner of both the Hitson Springs and the Bullhorn ranch headquarters, including their water rights. Also, these papers indicate that Mr. Canavan has also filed on the Thousand Springs area!"

"*What?*" Star Levitt's fingers gripped the arms of his chair and he half-rose. His plans ... All those carefully worked out plans were for nothing ... had always been for nothing. Whoever controlled water from those three sources controlled the Valley range, nor was there any way of circumventing it.

Pogue and Reynolds, whom he had destroyed, had never been the enemy. They had never owned anything, and had no more than a squatter's-rights claim on anything. He had not only been beaten, he had been made to look ridiculous.

"I told you," Canavan said quietly, "that you had overlooked the obvious. Somehow men of your stripe always do.

"Now, sir," Canavan continued. "With the cattle brands I can show you—one has only to skin a steer and look at the reverse side of the hide to see how they have been altered—I think you will understand what happened here.

"Star Levitt was anxious to get Miss Venable away, not only because he feared for her life when the shooting began, but because he did not want a witness to what was about to take place.

"Chubb picked a fight with young Riggs, and that shot was to open it. All of Levitt's men had pulled back into position, most of them with rifles. And when Chubb shot Riggs, that was the signal. And they opened up, killing Reynolds, Pogue, and whoever might oppose them or be witnesses."

"And you?" Clymer asked.

"I warned Mabry, and we got the hell out of there. We were supposed to be killed, too, but we got away. We had no part in the fight, and at that moment I did not actually know there was to be any shooting . . . I believed it, but I did not know. In any event, neither Pogue nor Reynolds would have believed me. They were so filled with jealousy and hatred of each other that they were blind to all else."

There was a slight stir at the back of the room, and glancing around, Canavan saw Emmett Chubb slipping out.

Star Levitt sat very still, his mind a blank. All his carefully thought out plans had been for nothing. He had been so sure, so confident. Now he had been shown up for both a fool and a murderer by the cowhand he despised. The name of murderer he could accept, but that of fool he could not.

Suddenly the rage that was in him exploded to madness. His face went white. His eyes bulging and glassy, he leaped from his chair and sprang for Canavan.

Warned by Dixie's scream, Bill Canavan jerked his eyes back from the vanishing Chubb and lunged to his feet to meet Levitt. Levitt's swinging right caught him on the cheek-bone and he staggered, driven back by the force of the larger man's onslaught. Bracing himself, he ducked under a left and swung a hard right to the body, but Levitt was insane with fury and frustration, and he came in swinging with both fists. Canavan buried a right in his mid-section, then hooked a bone-jarring left to the face.

Levitt clubbed a right to the back of the neck, but Canavan, veteran of many a rough-and-tumble cow-camp or mining-camp brawl, pulled his head away and bored in, smashing at Levitt's body with both fists. Levitt broke away, stabbed a left to the face and crossed with a right.

He was enormously powerful, yet a man who had boxed as well, and he knew what he was about. Canavan hit him again under the heart and, putting his head against Levitt's chest, backed him up several steps with powerful blows to the head and body. He felt Levitt's chin on his head, and jerked his own head up hard, butting him under the chin.

Suddenly, Levitt abandoned slugging and grappled with Canavan where he could use his strength to great advantage. Clasping his hands behind Canavan's back, he ground his knuckles into Canavan's spine. Canavan felt himself bent backward, further and further back. He felt a stab of excruciating pain, and in desperation he kicked up his feet and fell backward, bringing Levitt down on top of him. The sudden fall broke Levitt's hold, which was what he had hoped, and Canavan broke free, rolled over and came to his feet. He took a smashing blow to the head that staggered him. He felt his knees sag, but threw himself to the side to avoid the rush. Levitt leaped high and jumped to come down on his chest with both heels, but Canavan rolled over and kicked out hard with both boots. The kick caught Levitt on the thighs and knocked him off-balance. He fell hard, but started to his feet and was only half up when Canavan's right caught him in the mouth, knocking him back, his lips smashed into a bloody pulp mingled with fragments of broken teeth.

Canavan heard the sharp rap of a shot, and then another, but he was totally engrossed. Levitt plunged at him in a long driving tackle. Canavan lifted a knee in his face but went down himself.

Both men got up and Canavan, his endurance built from long hours in the saddle wrestling heavy steers, and working hard with his hands, was in the better shape. He moved in fast, stabbed a left to the face, then a right to the body. Levitt's breath was coming in great gasps. A right split his cheek, a left widened the cut. Suddenly, he turned and leaped through the window into the alley. Canavan caught a fleeting glimpse of Emmett Chubb with two horses. And then Chubb fired, and a bullet clipped the win-

dow frame behind his head, splattering him with
stinging splinters. And then they were gone.

A clatter of hoofs, and only silence.

Scott moved up to him and held out his guns. "I
wanted to get them to you sooner, but there was no
chance."

Clymer put a hand on his shoulder. "You've loyal
friends, Canavan. Burt and Mabry stopped the stage
outside of town after Levitt rode on ahead. They took
time to tell me a lot of things and to suggest that
we get you, Levitt and the Venables together and
withhold judgment until you had talked."

He shrugged. "It so happens that Neal and I
were both raised on stock ranches, and Mabry had
worked for both outfits at one time or another, so we
knew him for a good man and an honest one. So we
had some doubts as to Levitt's story. Mabry had a
cowhide with him, and any western man could see
that the brand had been altered from a VV to a Three
Diamonds.

"Just for the record, however, what happened
with Kerb Dahl?"

"I was suspicious about the unoccupied cabin
on the VV that was always watched, so I went there.
I found a cache of opium . . . a considerable amount,
actually. I hoped to have a word with Dixie Venable,
and went down to the house. Returning, I came face
to face with Dahl, and he asked me for a light, and
then recognized me almost at once. We both went
for our guns."

"He was said to be very good," Neal put in, curiously.

"Maybe he was. I never set myself up for a gunfighter although I've used guns all my life. But you
know how it is. For every known gunfighter around,
there are a dozen men who are just as good whom
you've never heard of. Maybe he was a mite slow that
night, maybe I was a little faster."

Later, Bill Canavan looked around for Dixie. She was standing outside the Cattleman's Café. He crossed over to where she stood. "Dixie? Why don't you go inside and order some coffee? I'll be along in a few minutes, and I'd like to talk to you."

"Bill? Be careful. He's filled with hatred, and he will not stop until he has killed you, or tried to. Be very careful!"

Mabry, Burt and Scott were waiting when he turned around, and they had his Appaloosa. "We can catch 'em, boss," Burt suggested, "but they've got quite a start."

"Later. I heard some shooting. What happened?"

"Voyle. He made a rush for his horse, tryin' to get away, an' he ran into Rolly. He figured Rolly would try to stop him so he grabbed for his gun, and he wasn't nearly so good as he thought."

"Tolman?"

"Roped an' hog-tied. The Rangers picked him up, and they got Turner, too. That Turner . . . no sand. He's been talkin' a'ready, enough to hang Levitt.

"Incidentally, I wanted to tell you about Scott an' Kinney. I ain't had time to talk to Scott, but I know what happened and how it happened. We moved down to May's like you said, and we seen you follered to Scott's by some of Levitt's outfit, so they had you pegged.

"They had us outnumbered and whilst we were tryin' to figure out what to do, Kinney came along. He said if he butted in he might keep you from being killed.

"That was my idea, too," Scott said. "When I let you in I saw there was somebody else out there, and had they been friendly they'd have come forward. So I seen that I had to make you my prisoner or they'd have us both, and as my prisoner I could protect you . . . up to a point."

"So Levitt, Chubb and Berdue are still loose?"

Mabry shook his head, with irritation. "That isn't

good, either, Canavan. Because if I know that lot, they'll not rest until they came back and kill you. You're going to have to be careful, take nothing for granted, and go armed and ready."

Yet as the days found their way down the year, and the summer faded toward autumn, there was no further sign of the three missing men. The mornings became chill and the aspen leaves turned from green to gold, mingled with the red of oak and sumac. The view from the growing house on the mesa changed, and sometimes in the early morning there was frost upon the grass.

A bank was robbed, then a stage looted and three men killed at Canyon Pass. And one passenger who survived had recognized one of the bandits as Emmett Chubb. Then the marshal in Pie Town was killed when he attempted to question a big, powerful man with a beard.

When Dixie rode through the Valley, Bill Canavan was constantly at her side, and the Appaloosa and Flame became companions. Despite the fact that few reports came from the three men, Canavan was worried.

"Bill," Dixie said, "you promised to take me to the crater in the lava beds. Why not today?"

He hesitated, thinking uneasily of the trail into the lava beds. "That place has me buffaloed," he admitted. "I never go in there but I wish that I was out. The way those big rocks hang over the trail will scare the daylights out of you. If one of them ever fell while we were in there, we'd likely never get out."

"At least we'd be together!" she reminded.

"That is an attraction," he admitted, "but I'd not want you confined in there all your life. Out here you can see a few other folks once in a while."

"But you've been there so many times, Bill! And Rolly tells me it is perfectly beautiful. I want to see the ice caves."

Below them there was a faint rumbling in the mountain, and they exchanged a glance. "I'm getting used to it now," he admitted. "But when I first heard it, that rumbling gave me the chills. When we move into the house, we'll have those holes fenced. They are really dangerous."

"I know. Ever since you told me about that awful hole, I've been frightened of it. I keep thinking of how awful it would be to be trapped down there, to get your foot caught in the rocks, or something like that. It would be frightful!"

"It would be the end!" Canavan agreed grimly. "When that geyser or whatever it is shoots up there, it sometimes brings rocks that must weigh fifty or sixty pounds. And they rattle around in that cave like seeds in a gourd. You wouldn't have to have a foot caught, either. All you would have to do is be just a few steps too far away from the mouth of the cave. You wouldn't have a chance!"

They were riding down the mesa through the aspens as they talked, the graceful trunks of the trees like slim, alabaster columns. The trail was carpeted with the gold of fallen leaves, and even as they rode other leaves came drifting down around them.

Dixie drew in at a wide place in the trail to look over the valley below. "Somehow it was like some dreadful dream," she said suddenly. "I mean when Star came. Tom and I had been so happy there on the ranch, really happy. We were working with the men, building some for ourselves and for the future, learning all the new things about the west. Tom loved working with stock, particularly the horses. And then, when we were happiest, Star Levitt came to the ranch.

"You can't imagine what a shock it was to us, for we believed all that had been left behind and forgotten. Our brother, the oldest one of the family, had gone to Mexico and gotten mixed up with a girl down there and started using dope. He'd always been father's favorite, and we all loved him, but Ralph had always been weak and easily led. Levitt got a hold on him and used his name for a front to peddle dope in the States.

"Father had been ill for a long time with a heart condition that grew steadily worse. He had just two things left to live for. One was pride of family, and the other was his children. Actually, that meant Ralph.

"We knew what had happened in Mexico and we knew about Star Levitt, but we kept it from Dad. And later, when Ralph was killed down there, we managed to keep the facts of the story from him. We knew the shock and the disgrace would kill him, and if by some chance he did live, the shame and disgrace would have ruined his last years. And he'd been a good father to us all.

"We were foolish, of course, but it is hard to know what to do in a situation like that, and one's very indecision works against one.

"Star came to the ranch and greeted us like long-lost friends. Then he told us he needed the ranch for a couple of months as a working base. He said he was no longer handling narcotics, only cattle. If he could use the ranch to hold his cattle for two months, then he would leave. If we did not consent, he promised he would get the news to our father, exposing the whole disgraceful affair and making sure our father heard it all.

"We were foolish, of course, but it was hard to know what to do. And when it came right down to it, there was nothing we could do. When he arrived, Emmett Chubb was with him. So was Kerb Dahl, and of course, that Turner. A few hours later, Voyle, Tolman and some others rode in.

"He simply moved in, took over, ran our honest hands off, and we were prisoners on our own ranch. They would never let us leave together unless they were with us. One of us was always kept at the ranch, so 'nothing foolish would be done,' as Star phrased it.

"There was nobody we could go to for help.

Pogue and Reynolds were fighting each other, but they themselves were outlaws, or but little better. Until you came, we were alone."

"Don't I know it?" Canavan commented. "When I heard about this place and started digging into the background, I found fewer decent people in this Valley than anywhere I'd ever been. And the few good people there were had no power. They were on small holdings or had small businesses, and the law almost never came up."

"After Star had been here a few weeks, he decided to stay. He was shrewd enough to know he could not keep on forever as he had been. He realized what was happening between Reynolds and Pogue and saw his chance to seize power and wealth. Just when we thought we were going to be rid of him, he decided to remain."

They rode on in silence then, their horses' hoofs making almost the only sound. Then suddenly they were opposite the entrance to the lava bed trail.

Dixie laughed. "All right, Bill! As long as we are here, why don't we ride in? We can be out before dark, as you said yourself!"

He hesitated, then turned Rio toward the lava beds. "All right," he said. "Have it your own way."

Yet he did not like it. And as he looked up at the towering cliffs, almost meeting overhead, he liked it even less.

He did not like to be trapped, and liked to go no place where he did not see another way out.

Even Dixie was quiet when she rode between the high, dark walls. A cool wind blew upon them, but she was not sure if it was the wind or the walls that made her shiver.

Rio, usually eager for any adventure, was reluctant. Yet they rode in. And went deeper and deeper into the dark, secret way.

All sound was left behind, and they could see

only a narrow strip of sky. Canavan swore softly . . . wishing he had not been so weak as to allow her to persuade him. He looked up, and the walls seemed to close above him like the jaws of some great monster.

Chapter XVIII

Once started into the narrow crevasse, there was no turning back. For much of the distance, there was no place with sufficient room to turn a horse. When they reached the deepest part, where in some bygone age an earthquake or some other great convulsion of the earth had split the rim of the crater deep into the bed-rock, Canavan pointed out the great crags suspended over the trail.

"Someday," he suggested, "this place will become inaccessible. Some earthquake, or perhaps even the jar of an explosion of some sort, and those rocks will fill this cleft so there will be no way out.

"From down here it looks as if a man with a bar could easily dislodge one of them. I never ride in here without getting the creeps at the thought. They are just laying up there, and need only the slightest jar to come roaring and tumbling down."

Tilting her head back, Dixie could see what he meant. And for the fisrt time she really understood Canavan's hesitation at bringing her in here, and she regretted her insistence. One great slab that must have weighed hundreds of tons seemed to be hanging suspended—for no reason she could make out.

It was an awesome feeling to be riding down here, with no sound but the click of their horses' hoofs, and with those enormous rocks suspended above them.

Once within the crater itself, Dixie forgot her fears in the excitement over the sheer beauty and grandeur of the place. The towering cliffs, the long sweeping meadows, the running stream and the great masses of clouds piled up over the mountains—all served to create the extraordinary sense of peace the place held.

It was warm and pleasant in the sunlight, and they rode without talking, just absorbing the beauty and the stillness. The red and brindle cattle had become more tame due to the frequency of the visits, and although wary, they seemed to welcome their presence.

"There were more cattle down here than I'd believed," Canavan said. "And there must be branch canyons and coves in the cliffs that I haven't seen. There's an old crater in northern New Mexico that is much greater than this one, although not as spectacular."

"Where are the ice caves? Rolly was telling me about the crystals."

For two hours they rambled around the crater, in and out of the ice caves. They found several caves where the cattle had been going to drink, and undoubtedly had occasionally taken shelter from storms. Suddenly, as they were about to leave, Dixie caught at Canavan's sleeve. "Bill! Look!"

It was a boot track, small but quite deep.

Her breath caught with fear. "Bill? It might be
... Could it have been Rolly Burt?"

"No, it wasn't Rolly." Mentally he was cursing
himself for ever having brought her here. "That foot
is smaller than either Mabry or Burt, and the man
who made it is heavier. Let's get out of here."

When they were out of the cave, he could see
the pallor of her face in the last of the sunlight. He
glanced at the sky, surprised at the sudden shadows
although it was drawing on toward the end of the
afternoon. Great, bulging thunderheads loomed over
the crater, piling up in ominous masses. It was going
to rain, and rain hard.

Leading the way, he started for the horses, every
sense alert. He saw no one. His movements started the
cattle drifting again, and as they reached the horses,
he told her, glancing at the sky, "You go ahead. I think
I'll start some more of the cattle while I'm at it."

"You can't do it alone!" she protested.

"I'll try. You head for home now. You'll get
soaked."

"Nonsense! I have my slicker, and—" her voice
faded and her eyes fastened on something beyond
Canavan's shoulder, widening with fear and shock.

He knew instantly what it was she saw, and for
one fleeting moment he considered drawing as he
turned. But he realized that Dixie would be right in
the line of fire.

"Really, you know," it was Star Levitt's voice, "this
is most opportune!"

It was Levitt's voice, all right, but there was
something in it that had a different tone, less of assurance and more than a hint of wildness. Something
perhaps like madness . . . or was he imagining things?
He turned slowly, and when his eyes met those of
Levitt he knew the worst.

All the neatness was gone. The white hat was
soiled and stained, his shirt was dirty, his face un-

shaved. He still had the large, really magnificent eyes, but now there was a light of insanity in them. Bill Canavan knew that the line that separates the sane from the insane had always been thinly drawn in this man. Defeat and frustration had been all that was needed to push him across the shadow-line.

"Oh, this is perfect!" Levitt said. "Today we will make a clean sweep! I get you, and later, Dixie! And while I am doing you in, Chubb and Berdue will finish off Mabry and Burt. They are up on the mesa now, waiting for them."

"On the mesa? They'll never surprise the boys there. Whenever one of us has not been on the mesa all day, we are extremely careful. We've been expecting you, Levitt."

"Have you now? Well, of course you have! But, you see, we found something you do not know. We found a cave up there, an ideal spot. And right there they will wait until they can catch your men off-guard tonight."

"A cave?" Canavan felt horror well up within him. His scalp prickled at the thought. Much as he disliked the two men, he had no wish to see any living thing trapped in that place. "A cave? You found a cave on the mesa?"

"We were all going to wait there until I saw you leaving with Dixie. It was too good a chance to miss. Besides," he glanced at Dixie, "I wanted her alone. She needs to be taught a lesson."

"Levitt," Canavan spoke quietly, "you are mad, you know? That cave where those men are hiding is a death trap! If they aren't within a few feet of the entrance, they haven't a chance to get out of there alive. Didn't you see that black hole in the center? That's a geyser, or something similar. Those men will be trapped and drowned!"

Levitt's smile vanished. "That's a lie, of course. But even if it isn't, it will not matter. I need them no longer, and Mabry and Burt . . . well, they are small-fry. It was you two that I wanted."

Canavan had shifted his position slightly and was now facing Levitt. He had done this simply by shifting his weight from one leg to the other, and moving his right foot a couple of inches in the process. It was all he needed.

His heart was pounding slowly, heavily. He knew he had no choice. He must draw and he must take a chance on beating Levitt to the shot. He himself would be hit, of that he was sure. But regardless of that, he must kill Star Levitt.

Wes Hardin and others had beaten men to the draw while covered, for there is such a thing as reaction time, and a split second could make all the difference. He knew how tremendously the odds were against him, but although he had never thought of himself as a fast man with a gun, he had beaten Kerb Dahl who was so considered.

He had also known of more than one man who had been shot through and through and had still continued to shoot, and accurately. And that was what he must do.

If he got out of this at all—and what was more important, if he got Dixie out of it—he could only do so by thinking clearer and acting with greater certainty. He would get hit. He faced that, accepted it, and fixed the idea in his mind that he would continue to shoot, and with care. This was one man he had to kill.

Thunder rumbled, and a few spattering drops of rain fell. His next remark came so casually, so naturally that even Star Levitt accepted it. "Better get your slicker, Dixie," he said cooly. "You'll get wet."

His eyes were riveted on Star Levitt, and what he waited for happened. As Dixie started to move, Levitt's eyes flickered for a fraction of an instant, and in that instant Bill Canavan went for his gun.

Levitt's gun flamed, but his eyes swung back and he shot too quickly, the bullet ripping by Canavan's head just as Canavan thumbed the hammer of his gun.

Once! . . . Again! He walked in on the big man intent only upon getting as much lead into him as possible. A bullet creased his arm and, involuntarily, he dropped his gun. Instantly he drew with his left hand . . . He wasn't quite as good with the left, but at this range . . .

Levitt's shirt was red with blood, and he fired into the red patch. Then he tilted the muzzle a fraction and put a round, blue hole at the base of Levitt's throat.

Yet the man wouldn't go down. He staggered, caught himself, started to bring his gun in line with Canavan's body. Cooly, Canavan took a step to the left, planted his foot solidly, and fired again and again.

Slowly, Levitt crumpled. He fell back on his left hand, staring up at Canavan with those magnificent eyes. "Next time I'll—!" The hand crumpled under him and he lay face up to the rain, eyes wide, unblinking.

Canavan turned sharply. "Get into that slicker! We've got to get out of here!"

The echoing of the gunfire died away and there was only the rain. He did not look at Levitt, simply turning away and picking up his dropped gun.

Dixie caught at him. "You're hurt! You're bleeding!"

"No time for that now." Surprisingly, he did not seem to be hurting, and felt no weakness. If he was hit . . . Of course, he had been hit on the arm . . . but it wasn't bothering him much. Something else was. He was thinking of the crevasse through which they must ride, and those great, hanging slabs.

Fighting his way into his slicker, he saw Dixie swing to the saddle and gallop out to make a swing around the cattle and start them toward the opening.

Surprisingly, the big steer who took the lead headed into the crack as if it had done so before, and in fact many of the cattle must have fed both in and outside the crater.

Waving Dixie ahead of him, he followed her into the cleft, casting scared glances aloft. He grabbed a stone off a small ledge and hurled it at a laggard cow. "Get going!" he yelled, and pushed hard. The cattle were moving, moving too slowly.

Suddenly, something . . . somewhere, started them moving faster, then faster. Now they were running, and Dixie's horse was scrambling at the rocks right behind them.

He glanced up as they neared the narrowest part. Horror filled him, for that great, hanging slab had seemed to move!

"*Hurry!*" he yelled. "Use your rope! Keep them running!"

Dixie glanced up and he saw her face as a white, scared blotch in the driving rain. A thin trickle of stones fell, splashing into the cleft, and pools of water were gathering here and there. Canavan looked up again, and this time there was no doubt. The great slab moved, grated horribly against the rock beneath, and sent another trickle of stones ahead to scout the path. The rock started to move again, hesitated, then its great table-top inclined almost majestically. And with gathering speed, it started to slide!

Shale and gravel rattled down the cliff, and his horse leaped forward, pushing against Flame. And Flame in turn pushed against the laggard steer. It leaped ahead, and Flame scrambled after. With shouts and yells he urged the cattle on, and with a coiled rope Dixie lashed out at the nearest. They began to trot again, then to run. From behind them came a great reverberating roar and, turning in the saddle, he glanced back.

He was somewhat higher now, out of the worst of the cleft, and he could see the great rock slide the last of its distance to the sheer edge, pushing rocks and boulders before it. Then, on the very lip, it held itself, balanced for a breathless instant and then it fell. It struck somewhere far below, and there was a great rush of air up the cleft in the rock. Rio leaped nervously, and tugged at the bit to get on. Now the whole side seemed to be sliding down into the crevasse.

On a small open space where the cleft widened at a somewhat higher level, they drew up and sat their saddles in the rain, looking back. "It's a tomb," she said, "a tomb wide open to the sky. Nobody will ever find him now."

"The wolves will," he said, "and the cougars."

She shuddered. "What an awful thing! Do you suppose it is really closed?"

Canavan shrugged. "There may have been some other way. I never had the time to look. Or maybe a man who was a good rock climber could get in . . . or out. I wouldn't try it."

The pounding rain beat upon their hats and their shoulders, and they drove the cattle slowly out upon the widening plain, then left them and started for the mesa.

Canavan thought of his guns, and one by one he reloaded them, returning them to their holsters. He had started packing two six-shooters when he rode shotgun on the stage. For a man might need firepower against a sudden attack by Indians or outlaws, yet it was the first time since those days that he had had any use for that second gun.

Burt ran from the cabin as they rode up, taking their bridles. "Get inside an' get dry!" he yelled. "We've been worried about you two!"

When they were inside with their slickers off and hot coffee in their cups, Burt said, "Mabry thought he saw Chubb earlier today. We were worried about you."

"You haven't seen them?" Canavan paused with his cup halfway to his lips.

Burt had come in, hearing the question. He took off his slicker and hung it on a peg. "No, an' I'll be just as pleased if I never see them again."

He took a cup and filled it from the blackened pot. "This here rain must be playing tricks with that geyser. I was over thataway when she boiled up, and I'd of sworn it sounded like a human, screeching down in there. Made the hair stand on my neck! You know, I—" He paused. "What's the matter? What did I say?"

Dixie had turned quickly away, going into the inner room. Rolly looked after her, puzzled. "What's wrong? I mean—"

"Forget it, Rolly. And don't mention that geyser again."

Slowly, he related the events of the day. The ride into the lava beds, the end of Star Levitt, and the slide that closed . . . or apparently closed . . . the cleft.

"Was he sure-enough dead?" Mabry asked. "You real sure?"

"I'm sure. Rain was falling into his wide-open eyes."

Dixie returned to the room. "Bill, those poor men! Trapped in that awful place! They were cruel, vindictive men, but I'd wish that on nobody."

"Forget about it. They were hiding there to kill us." He put his hand on her arm. "Look, honey, at the fire. It is our fire, in our home! Smell that coffee Mabry has on? And listen to the rain! That rain means that the grass will be tall and green when spring comes again to the Valley, green on our hills, and for our cattle!"

They stood together watching the dance of the flames and listening to the thunder of the rain on the roof, hearing the great drops that fell down the chimney hiss out their anguish in the coals. A stick fell, a blaze crept along it, feeling hungrily for places to burn.

Dishes rattled in the kitchen, and Rolly was pouring coffee.

ABOUT THE AUTHOR

Louis L'Amour, born Louis Dearborn L'Amour, is of French-Irish descent. Although Mr. L'Amour claims his writing began as a "spur-of-the-moment thing," prompted by friends who relished his verbal tales of the West, he comes by his talent honestly. A frontiersman by heritage (his grandfather was scalped by the Sioux), and a universal man by experience, Louis L'Amour lives the life of his fictional heroes. Since leaving his native Jamestown, North Dakota, at the age of fifteen, he's been a longshoreman, lumberjack, elephant handler, hay shocker, flume builder, fruit picker, and an officer on tank destroyers during World War II. And he's written four hundred short stories and over fifty books (including a volume of poetry).

Mr. L'Amour has lectured widely, traveled the West thoroughly, studied archaeology, compiled biographies of over one thousand Western gunfighters, and read prodigiously (his library holds more than two thousand volumes). And he's watched thirty-one of his westerns as movies. He's circled the world on a freighter, mined in the West, sailed a dhow on the Red Sea, been shipwrecked in the West Indies, stranded in the Mojave Desert. He's won fifty-one of fifty-nine fights as a professional boxer and pinch-hit for Dorothy Kilgallen when she was on vacation from her column. Since 1816, thirty-three members of his family have been writers. And, he says, "I could sit in the middle of Sunset Boulevard and write with my typewriter on my knees; temperamental I am not."

Mr. L'Amour is re-creating an 1865 Western town, christened Shalako, where the borders of Utah, Arizona, New Mexico, and Colorado meet. Historically authentic from whistle to well, it will be a live, operating town, as well as a movie location and tourist attraction.

Mr. L'Amour now lives in Los Angeles with his wife Kathy, who helps with the enormous amount of research he does for his books. Soon, Mr. L'Amour hopes, the children (Beau and Angelique) will be helping too.